LEN WORLD

ISOBEL WYCHERLEY

Dedicated to Liam Roscoe and his wonderful, supportive family.

ACKNOWLEDGMENTS

Thank you, again, to my sister who always keeps a close eye on my writing and gives me feedback to help me improve my skills. She has believed in me from day one, and inspires me to keep going. I would also like to thank the extremely talented Lorna Read, who reached out to tell me how much she enjoyed my first book, Gone Too Far West. This gave me the confidence I needed to really pursue this dream, she gave me so much support and advice throughout writing this book, I really couldn't have done it without her.

It would be rude of me not to acknowledge the man behind the Len, Liam Roscoe. Although reading isn't his forte, he still keeps up with my writing and constantly assures me of how proud he is, which also contributes to my determination to continue doing what I love.

And, of course, thank you to anybody who buys my books or simply supports them- friends, family and strangers I've met on nights out, I couldn't do it without you either.

INTRODUCTION

Today is an exciting day for the people who dedicate their lives to confining people who are failed and rejected by society. Their pristine white plimsolls squeak in unison as they march down the empty hall, single file, eager to know what they have all been summoned to the staffroom for. Nobody knows who has called them here, but, as they flow into the room, they know he means business because of his shiny new briefcase and squinty, Clint Eastwood eyes that analyse them, one by one, as they slump down into their seats. Silence fills the room as they wait impatiently for him to speak.

"Hello. Thank you all for coming," he begins, his booming voice spreading to every inch of the room, filling it with noise.

Just as they'd hoped.

"I am Detective Reinhold, and this is my partner, Detective Shelley." He holds out a gorilla-sized hand to present the haggard old man beside him, slouched against the table, with his arms folded across his thin body.

Together, they look like a before and after shot of a raging alcoholic. The 'before' being an honourable man, every feature big and distinguished, all held together with pride. The 'after', a frail shell of a man, with more bags than Paris Hilton, his cracked and sagging body breaking a little bit more with every painful step.

"We've gathered you here in order to brief you all about your new tenant arriving tomorrow," he starts to explain. "Some of you may already know of him –"

"Ooh! Is it Charles Manson?" a young nurse called Paul, with a kind face and thin black hair, interrupts.

Reinhold wonders how someone so stupid has managed to get a job like this. "No. And I do not take kindly to interruptions. There will be time at the end for questions. For now, you need to listen very carefully to what I am going to tell you."

Paul hangs his head in childish shame as Reinhold continues.

"The patient in questions is called Len Moscow. You may recognise his name from a number of national news outlets. If you are unaware, he is one of four suspects in the murder case of Gaz Neugent, who was brutally killed in the summer of 2018. The thing that makes Len so special is that he is the only living suspect."

The nurses look around nervously at each other.

"There have been a number of stories emerging about what happened on the night of the murder. But one thing we know for certain is that Len and his three friends were the last people to see Gaz alive and, ultimately, deceased. Thanks to one suspect, Flic, who wrote her account of the night in question, in a book called *Gone* –"

"– *Gone Too Far West*! Oh my God, I LOVE that book!" Paul interrupts again, instantly regretting his reaction.

"Well then... Perhaps you can explain it to everyone," Reinhold spits through gritted teeth.

All the while, Shelley stares glumly at the floor, unaffected by anything being said, almost as if he isn't listening to a word.

"Okay..." Paul rises from his chair, hoping to prove himself to Reinhold. "Soooo... They were in a park. At night. Tripping on drugs. Aaaand, Gaz comes over. Creeps them out... He walks off into the forest... Later, they hear a commotion. They investigate, but they all see a different murder scene playing out in front of them. So, basically, no one knows what really happened-"

"*WRONG!*" Reinhold bellows. The interruptee becomes the interrupter.

The nurses jump in surprise – especially Paul, who has cowered back down into his seat. Some of them stifle their laughter behind sweaty palms.

"Len knows what happened," Reinhold continues, "And it is down to you lot to find out what he knows. If you do... you will be *very* generously rewarded."

Worried faces transform into devious smirks as their interest is freshly replenished.

"But at the end of the book, Flic says she was the one who did it," Paul quizzes from the safety of his seat.

"We know. But we checked out that lead and it doesn't seem to fit the evidence," Reinhold explains. "We've exhausted all of our systems, and we still cannot get to the bottom of this case. This is our final option. We've bugged his room and we'll send a body language specialist in every day, undercover as another patient. He'll take on the role of the poker dealer in order to detect any deceptive behaviour that Len might show. But, additionally we need you to use your 'techniques'," he mimes quotation marks with his thick fingers, "in order to get the truth out of him."

Everyone acknowledges that this equates to 'by any means necessary', including their more unethical approaches.

"I have a question..." A fat nurse with a deep, raspy voice, at the back of the room, raises her chubby arm in the air. It looks like a joint of beef, her rolls secured with thin pieces of string, keeping the tender meat intact as it cooks in its own juices.

"Go on," Reinhold directs.

"Why is he being sent here, of all places?" she huffs. Lifting her arm is enough exercise for today.

"Because, sir – er, miss, sorry – he's been fabricating delusional stories about the murder and events surrounding it. He's been deemed mentally unstable and is now a potential suspect. There is no better place for him than here, especially given your reputation."

So, where is 'here'? Well, I'll tell you. 'Here' is George Lee's Psychiatric Hospital, one of the last ones of its kind. It was built in the 1600s, for the exact same purpose as it's used for today: detaining a group of people that we cannot, or will not, help. Situated across three floors and a basement, each level has its own purpose. The ground floor holds the dayroom, where all patients can mix with each other under the unwatchful eye of the horrendous nurses, as well as the food hall. The first floor is where the female patients sleep and shower, the second floor being for the men; both of these have a communal area, for those that do not wish or are not allowed to mix with the opposite sex. I can't bring myself to tell you what the basement is for. The building has a barbaric history, but brutality is not left solely in the past like it should be... Something that will become clear to you, and our poor boy, Len.

Shelley distributes a copy of *Gone Too Far West* to every nurse, so they know what they're getting themselves in to. Reinhold begins to wrap up the meeting as they flick through the pages and examine the cover.

"I want you all to read this by tomorrow morning, in advance of your new arrival. We will return at the end of every week to check in with you all. However, if you have any information prior to our meetings, do not hesitate to contact either me or Detective Shelley."

Shelley slowly turns to face them again as he makes it back to the front of the room. He gives them a gentle nod, his tired eyes full of hope, longing for the moment when this case can be closed.

The investigators bid their farewells and the nurses return to their night-time duties before returning home themselves. Apprehensive about the week ahead.

CHAPTER ONE

6 am: time to wake up the patients. An alarm that cuts through the bone is blasted out of hundreds of speakers dotted around the building. They drag themselves out of bed, with a little help from the nurses, brush their teeth and are all ushered to the showers. Freezing cold, as always.

The men pull on their blood-red overalls and make their way to the communal room at the end of their dorm. They're surprised to see a circle of chairs in the middle of the room with a nurse stationed behind every one.

"Come in." A tall male doctor with glasses and a long white lab coat gestures with his hands for them to sit down.

He's the head of the ward, Doctor Harris, a man who is seldom seen wandering around, mixing with patients. Something big must be happening. He has an air of respect hanging around him. Quiet, but confident. Modest, yet conceited. A recluse, who nevertheless has a way with people.

With caution, the patients sit, twisting their necks to look up at the nurses behind them.

"There's nothing to worry about," Doctor Harris reassures them, sensing their hesitation to join them in the circle. "We have a new, very interesting, patient joining us today. So, we thought we'd give him our biggest welcome." He smiles.

It's unsure whether his joyfulness and affection for the patients is genuine or not. But who cares? He has treated them better in these mere few moments than any of the nurses ever have.

One patient speaks out. "Who is he?"

"Well, I'm glad you asked that, Mehzah. He'll be sharing a room with you!" Doctor Harris chirps.

Mehzah curses under his breath as some of the patients snigger at him. It's a luxury to have your own room in a place like this, but very rare. It is said that Mehzah coaxed his last roommate into committing suicide so that he could have the room to himself. They questioned him but, quiet as always, he just stuck his many chins out at them. Nothing was conclusive.

"Now, now. I want you all to make him feel welcome, like he's part of the family."

Before anyone can mock the use of the word 'family', the double doors, windows covered with thick wire mesh, are swung open. A nervous-looking young man is escorted into the room by two nurses either side of him, each with a hand under his arms, just in case they need to drag him anywhere.

"Ah! Speak of the Devil. Everybody, this is your new friend, Len Moscow." Doctor Harris introduces him to everybody.

Len looks around at all of the unamused and overly amused faces that stare back at him, making him even more nervous.

"Oh my God, Len! It's such an honour to meet you!" Paul runs over to him, *Gone Too Far West* clutched in his shaking hand.

"Get a grip of yourself, sir," Doctor Harris says to him in an unusually calm manner.

Paul drops his head and retreats backwards to where he stood before. A smirk forms across Len's lips. He's a celebrity!

Soon enough, he gains his confidence, greeting everyone individually, shaking hands, patting some patients on the shoulder as he chats. Len sits down on the last remaining chair and folds his right leg over the left, hands clasped tightly on his knee. He smiles. He's quite happy with himself.

"So, Len. Welcome to George Lee's hospital. We hope you will find your time here to be pleasant and worthwhile," Doctor Harris starts, trying to make the stay sound voluntary.

"Thanks, thanks." Len holds a hand up to wave to his subjects.

"Why don't you tell us a little bit about yourself?" As Doctor Harris says this, all of the nurses whip out their notepads and pens, ready to start when the klaxon sounds.

Ready. Set. Go.

"Hi, I'm Len, as you all know. I'm twenty years old, and I'm a murder suspect from Warrington." A line that would not have gone down well if he'd been on a gameshow.

Paul makes sure to note this all down with his special navy-blue, tortoiseshell pen, inscribed with his name, that his mother bought him for Christmas: you never know, he thinks; if he solves the case, these precious notes might sell for a fortune in a few years' time.

"A murder suspect, wow! What happened?" Mehzah's eyes light up. Another of his kind.

"Well, it's all a bit of a mix-up, really. You see..." he begins.

"It was a crazy year. I spent the whole time with my mates, Flic, Javan and Jenkies. Flic had this beautiful black ship called Black Beauty, which I had just been promoted to Captain of. I woke up one morning, I could hear my name being called. It was the crew. I emerged from underneath the deck to a raging storm. But not of wind and rain. Of cannonballs! We gave it our best effort to fight back, of course. But the ship was captured, by none other than Blackbeard himself! He had piercing blue eyes, sharper than his sword! Scars on his face were deeper than the ones he had made to our ship!"

By now, the nurses had removed the tips of their pens from the paper and instead watched him, irritatingly, dance around the circle, acting out his fantasies. Some of the patients follow him around with their wide-open eyes, yearning to hear what happens next.

"I couldn't just stand there and watch my crew be killed. As soon as he stepped foot on my ship, I swung around the boat on one of the ropes and pierced him directly in the heart, through his back. He never saw me coming. I was hailed a hero by my shipmates and everyone else, but authorities saw it differently..."

"What happened to Black Beauty?" an older patient shouts to Len eagerly.

"I fixed it, of course. With my bare hands." He holds them up for everyone to ogle over.

The old man, known only as Mr Lewis, reaches out a frail hand to connect his with Len's.

"Eh! Look, don't touch." Len pulls his hand away.

Doctor Harris rolls his eyes quickly before anyone can see. "Alright. Well, I think that's enough for today..." He glances at the nurses. "Mehzah, why don't you show Len to your room and give him a quick tour of the facilities. Introduce him to some more of the patients." He walks over to the big nurse, the one who physically enforces the rules of the institute and they whisper to each other.

This nurse, we have met before. The harsh, obese woman called Mrs Hunning. Known to patients as Atilla the Hun. She is strict and unforgiving, and in no way shy about it. That's why they hired her.

She steps forward, presenting herself to the circle of the forgotten.

"Right, you 'eard the man! Everyone else get to your usual business!"

CHAPTER TWO

"This is our room." Mehzah ushers Len inside the tiny room.

He takes a look around, despite there being nothing in the room except for two metal beds bolted to the floor. Len notices a pile of comic books on Mehzah's bed and he sees him looking at them.

"You can get magazines delivered here," says Mehzah. He walks over and picks up the one on top of the pile. "This is my favourite one, *The Adventures of Sewer Boy*, it's very exciting." He holds the cover up for Len to see.

A man dressed in rubbish bags and a scraggly hat, stood in the sewer with his hands on his hips. Interesting...

"I'd learn how to sleep with one eye open if I were you, bru. Gets dangerous here at night," Mehzah whispers, as he shuffles closer to Len.

Len stares back. "I'm sure I'll be fine. Can we go and see what's downstairs?" he urges.

"Yes." Mehzah turns around slowly and walks down the

corridor to the stairwell. "There's the dayroom and the cafeteria down here. Where all the fun happens, innit."

Exiting the stairwell, to the right, two giant doors are held open to display a giant dayroom, full of patients. Big, stained-glass windows cover the room in red and pink. An old TV set supplies entertainment to the group of people huddled together on chairs and sofas. A ping-pong table sits over by the wall, untouched all day. Len spots a scrum of people hanging around the corner of the room.

"What's going on over there?" Len asks Mehzah.

He panics. "I wouldn't go over there, bru, that's Big Al."

"Who's Big Al?"

"The most feared patient in here! Even the nurses are scared." He begins to shake.

"Come on, he can't be that bad."

Len begins to walk over to the crowd. He turns around to see if Mehzah is following, but he's completely disappeared.

Guess I'm going in alone.

He pushes patients out of the way to see what's so interesting. A green table, covered in packs of cigarettes and crumpled pieces of paper, a straight line of cards running down the middle, is surrounded by patients who are sitting on wooden chairs, holding playing cards close to their chests.

"Fold!" one patient cries, thumping his fist on the table, his black, matted hair covering his tears.

Everyone goes silent for a while...

"Scott!" someone shouts, awakening a young man adorned with a blond mullet.

He snorts as he sits back up in his chair, a card stuck to his cheek with drool. He peels it off, takes a quick glance. "All in." He pushes his pack of cigarettes into the middle.

Len looks at the cards spread out across the table: queen of hearts, ace of diamonds, ace of hearts, king of hearts and eight of diamonds.

He must have a full house.

"All right..." The dealer collects the last round of bets. "Show your hands."

Scott puts his hand down first, ace of clubs, king of diamonds. "Full house!" He smirks.

"Oh, nice! Al, what've you got?" The dealer says.

Which one's Al?

"Royal flush." A jack and ten of hearts is gently placed on the table.

A small girl, blonde hair plaited innocently on the back of her head, wearing a dark green turtle neck under her red overalls, smiles as she collects her winnings. The table erupts into mayhem. Some praising the winner and the exciting game, others cursing to themselves, having lost.

"How did I lose that?" Scott throws his cards to the dealer.

"Better luck next time, Scotty." Big Al winks at him as she stands up from the table, putting her winnings in her pocket.

She glances at Len, hidden amidst the crowd. His heart skips a beat but he manages to stay composed.

As the group begins to thin, he stands his ground. The only people left are the dealer, Scott, Big Al, the patient with matted hair and, of course, Len.

"And who might you be?" Big Al asks, without smiling.

"Eh? I'm Len. I arrived this morning," he struggles to say.

"Nice to meet you, I'm Al. This is Scott Green," she gestures to the mullet, "this is Theo," she then gestures to the sad-looking one, "and this is The Dealer."

He nods at Len.

"Hi." Len nods back.

"So, what are you in here for?" Scott asks, looking up at Len.

"I'm not sure..." He fumbles for words.

"Well, I'm sure we'll find out soon enough." Big Al claps her hands together, triggering everyone else to get up from the table.

Len backs away from them, unsure of what this implies.

Al starts towards him, walking swiftly around the table. Len freezes in fear. She hits him hard on the back, pulling him in closer towards her.

"Do you smoke, Len?" she asks. Scott and Theo are closing in on him now as well.

"Eh? Smoke what?" he replies.

The three of them erupt into enormous laughter,

"That's a yes then!" Scott roars over their howls.

Len tries to giggle along, his eyes darting between the three of them. They all stop laughing suddenly, and so does Len.

"Stick with us, mate. You'll find that loony bins aren't as bad as you think." Al laughs and Scott and Theo chuckle to each other, too.

I've done it. I'm in!

CHAPTER THREE

"Have you had the grand tour, then?" Big Al asks Len.

"Mehzah showed me a little bit. I haven't seen everything though," he replies.

"All right. Well, that's the poker table, obviously. Do you like poker?"

"Yeah, it's all right." He lies, he loves poker.

"We're only allowed one game a day, otherwise everyone would be on the bones of their arse. Look at this," she takes a crumpled piece of paper out of her pocket and smoothes it out, "someone's bet their soul... Mine now."

"That was me," Theo speaks up.

She looks at him and shakes her head, a smile creeping out of the corner of her mouth. She crumples the paper back up and throws it at him. Theo juggles it around in his hands as he tries not to drop it.

"Careful!" he shouts.

"That's the ping-pong table, nobody plays it," Big Al states.

"Why not?"

"You see that old man there? Mr Lewis?" She points at him as he sits watching the TV.

"Yeah."

"He kept eating the ping-pong balls."

"Why?" Len laughs, not sure if she's joking.

"Because they're far more delicious than what he gets served here." She chuckles, Scott and Theo joining in, too.

They walk over to the TV, to introduce everyone to Len.

"Hello everyone," Big Al greets the inmates who are gathered around the box.

"Hi, Big Al!" everyone chirps back, staggering their replies to make sure they're all heard by her.

"This is our new mate, Len. Len, this is Mr Lewis."

"We've met! Wonderful boy!" Mr Lewis sings, his arms stretched out like he's in an opera.

Mr Lewis hasn't always been crazy. He left school at thirteen to join the army to fight in the Second World War, so he's never been the brightest bulb, but he has a lot of passion and enthusiasm. Two days before the war ended, he was discharged with shell-shock and sent here. He's delusional still, and often has nightmares about his time on the battlefield. He lost all of his hair from the stress, pulling out every last strand, and his body shakes constantly, he can't help it, like a restless little boy trapped in an old man's body.

"This is Eucalyptus."

"Hi, Len!" A young girl, with brown hair so long that it disappears under her bum, is sitting crossed-legged on the floor. She stands up to give Len a hug.

She's barefooted as well, he notices and her jumpsuit is opened as far as it can go, to display her skinny chest with bones protruding from anywhere they can. Her face is pretty, covered in tiny freckles; she has a big, wide smile and eyes that look like they hold the knowledge of the entire world. Brought up in a cult in the countryside of Wales, it's no wonder she ended up in here. She talks about all the good times, living off the land, bathing in rivers and breeding their own animals. What she doesn't tell you is that her mother rented her out to older men in the cult from the day Eucalyptus was born, until the day she finally plucked up the courage to kill her own mother. That's when she got diagnosed with bipolar I and was sent to George Lee's Hospital.

"This is DJ Gurns." Big Al motions to the guy over by the TV who is twisting the volume and channel knobs and bopping his head violently to his imaginary tune.

"*HEY DUDE! DO YOU LIKE THE TUNE?*" he shouts over his music.

Len looks at Al for an answer.

"Just say yeah," she whispers to him.

"Yeah! Love it." Len bobs his head to match in time with DJ Gurns' rhythm.

Nobody really knows much about DJ Gurns apart from the fact that he can't control his volume and is always shouting over the tunes blasting in his head. When he's not twisting knobs, he's sitting in a chair, staring blankly in front of him, with a thin flow of dribble coming out from his mouth and nothing behind his eyes. His bottom jaw swings helplessly on its own with no control and no destination in mind. He has the strangest case of catatonia anyone has ever seen, almost as if he switches between the retarded and excited type. But honestly, God only knows what's up with that boy.

"And that squinty-eyed fuck over there is Randall Savage." Al points an accusing finger at a man hunched over behind everyone, a notepad in his hand.

He quickly scribbles something down in it. "Squinty-eyed fuck over there," he repeats. "I'm telling Mrs Hunning about that!" he snarls.

"I don't doubt that you will, mate," Al replies, rolling her eyes.

"Snitches get stitches, Randall!" Scott shouts over to him.

Nobody likes Randall Savage, the hospital snitch. His eyes are so squinty and creepy that even his hairline has receded as far back away from them as it can. He's got the body to match, a curved spine making him constantly hunched, and long spindly hands, one with an extra finger, so he can point out and snitch on six people at once with just one hand.

They stroll into the empty food hall that is being prepared for lunchtime. A couple of nurses set out the tables and chairs around the room, whilst the kitchen staff sweat over their big, metal cauldrons. The nurses wave at Al silently, and she clicks her fingers into the shape of a gun at them. They walk into the kitchen area, hot and humid with the heat of whatever's cooking.

"Are we allowed in here?" Len asks.

"*We* are." Big Al smiles at him and raises her eyebrows.

"All right, Cookie. What's on the menu today?" Scott asks the shrivelled old cook, whose teeth are dangerously close to falling into the food she slaves over.

"Sssoup!" She spits into it.

The four of them groan and laugh at the sight of it.

"But for yoooou," she sings, walking over to the fridge and opening the door, "I made sssomething extra ssspecial."

They walk over to the fridge to look. A full chicken is sat glistening, shiny in its plastic wrapping and ready to eat.

"Oof, what's accompanying it?" Scott licks his lips.

"I've got sssome roasted ssspudsss, veg, and my ssspecial gravy," she lists.

"Ooooh, dirty bastard! I CANNOT wait for that, Cookie, you're a star, I tell ya!" Big Al praises, as she kisses her on her wrinkly old cheeks.

"Anything for my favouritesss!" She smiles, revealing the gums of her loose dentures.

"This is our new mate, Len, by the way. So, you're gonna have to cook for one more in future." Theo speaks for the first time in ages and sounds surprisingly authoritative as well.

Cookie walks over to Len and pinches his cheeks with greasy fingers.

"Anything for a handsssome young man!" She smiles, inches away from his face.

He closes an eye and leans his face to the side to dodge as much spit as possible, making sure to keep his mouth closed.

"Alright! Put him down, cougar!" Al laughs. "We're gonna go upstairs for a smoke and we'll eat when we come down, is that all right?" she asks Cookie.

"Of coursssse, my dear. I'll have it ready for you all." She pats Al on the cheek now, like a loving grandmother.

"Thanks, Cookie," everyone says, as they make their way through a hidden door behind the fridges, and up the tiny stairwell to the roof.

They reach a heavy, red fire exit door that has a normal handle rather than the long rails.

Scott pushes it but it doesn't budge.

"Locked," he says, but doesn't sound defeated.

Al unzips the breast pocket of her overalls and pulls out a little key, holding it up to Len. "Open sesame!" She smiles, and pushes it into the lock.

Scott tries the handle again and the door swings open, displaying an unimaginable view of the town, the sun steady in the middle of the clear, baby-blue sky. Not a cloud in sight.

"Whoa... how did you get that key?" Len asks, after admiring the view.

"Dr Harris gave it to me," she says, as if it's nothing.

"What! Why?" Len puzzles.

"You don't need to know, mate." She winks.

There are three deck chairs already laid out, facing the beautiful landscape. Theo grabs another one that's leaning against the wall and sets it out for Len.

They sit down and Scott pulls out a long spliff from a packet of cigarettes and lights it.

"Where did you get that from?" Len asks again, bewildered at what they manage to get away with.

"You ask a lot of questions, Len," Scott says, as he breathes the smoke out.

"That, you have no business knowing the answer to," Theo pipes up.

Len says nothing, just looks around and decides to enjoy it rather than constantly question what's going on.

"Go easy on him, guys. It's his first day, remember?" Big Al says and smiles at Len, once she catches his gaze.

They smoke the spliff without saying much to each other and get up to leave. Making sure to lock the door again behind them, they walk back into the kitchen where Cookie is standing there waiting for them.

"Dinner is ssserved!" she performs.

They all thank her again and wander further into the kitchen, to a little room at the back. A nicely set table with four plates overflowing with a full chicken dinner awaits them.

CHAPTER FOUR

L en's first night at the hospital was uneventful, and a full tummy made sure he was comatose until morning, even sleeping through the alarm. He wakes up dazed, on a hard white mattress, wrapped up only in a thin white sheet and the watchful eyes of Mehzah. Remembering that he wasn't at home anymore, Len jolts up to a seated position, hitting the nape of his neck on the metal headboard in the process. He rubs it gently as he finally calms down and meets Mezah's gaze.

"All right?" Len huffs.

"How did yesterday go?" Mezah whispers. Len has to lean closer to hear him.

"Good. Big Al's actually really nice."

"You spoke to her?" He almost shouts. It's the loudest thing he's ever said.

"Yeah, we're friends now."

"Oh no. This is bad." Mehzah begins to pace back and forth through the tiny room, muttering to himself.

"Why?... Why?... Why?" Len swings his legs off the bed and tries to get in Mehzah's face for him to hear his question.

"Don't you know who she is?" he snarls quickly, very close to Len's face.

"No," Len whispers back.

Before he can answer, a shadow from the doorway is cast over them.

"Sorry to interrupt your intimate moment, boys. It's meeting time," a tall, muscular nurse called Adesso shouts into them.

This was not Adesso's first choice of career. He wanted to be a police warden, strong and feared. Finally, he could be the one to violently enforce rules onto other people, like they had done to him all his life. Unfortunately, he got into some trouble with the law in his teenage years, and was unable to join the police force. So, here he is. He lets his anger and frustration boil up inside of him, until something happens that gives him a just reason to explode. The purest form of release for him.

Mehzah straightens up and follows Adesso into the communal room at the end of the hall. Len throws on his overalls, skipping the shower, and joins everybody in the circle.

Dr Harris isn't there today, the meeting is led by Atilla.

"Good morning, everybody. Len, it's nice of you to join us at last." She raises her eyebrow at him.

"Sorry. I was exhausted." He rubs his eyes with his thick fingers.

"Not to worry. I expect to see you with all the other patients tomorrow morning, however. Bright 'n' early," she says, no meaning behind the first set of words.

"I will be." Len nods.

"Good. Now..." She moves on, taking her notepad out from her front pocket. "Today, we're going to talk about turning points. What happened to get you to this point? Mr Lewis, maybe you'd like to kick-start the session." She looks at him intently.

"Well... I think the turning point for me was..." he hesitates. "... was when I saw my best friend shot dead right in front of me. I could have saved him, but my gun jammed. They were temperamental things in those days. I got it working in time to save myself, though..." He stares off at the floor, thinking deeply about something. Then his eyes start to jump around the room and he looks more and more panicked.

"Did you want to save him?" Atilla asks – perhaps stoking the fire to intimidate Len.

"Of course I wanted to save him!" Mr Lewis howls. "He was my best friend! We were just kids!" he preaches, as tears flow out of his eyes, like a tap on full blast.

"Calm down, Mr Lewis." Atilla rolls her eyes, unimpressed with his ridiculous outburst.

The nurses surround him and wrap a belt around his arms to keep him static like an ironing board, and they sit him back down.

"No one could save him!" he wails.

"You could've," she states.

Mr Lewis can no longer answer through his pain. It's hard to watch.

"All right, stop it! Stop it now! Leave the old man alone!" Len shouts, but not to Atilla, to everyone.

Mr Lewis hears, and controls his howls to short sobs and sniffles. His blue eyes look lovingly at Len, his hero.

"You're making him worse." Len's voice softens as he makes eye contact with a very unsympathetic Atilla.

"Okay then, Len. Why don't you take over? And tell the truth this time." She smirks and looks at the others nurses, who have now left Mr Lewis to crumble into himself.

"My turning point was the death of my best friends... and my girlfriend." He starts off strong, until he thinks about Flic.

"And how did they die, Mr Moscow? Did you kill them?" Atilla taunts him.

"No." He almost loses his temper before realising that's what she wants. "It was all a freak accident."

"What happened?" Mr Lewis croaks, feeling a connection with him, having both lost their friends too young.

"Well..." he starts, "my friend, Jav, was the first to go. We weren't with him at the time, he committed suicide."

Atilla writes this down, feeling like she's finally made progress with Len.

"Then it was Jenk's turn... We weren't supposed to be there. We weren't supposed to be smoking what we were, either. But everyone was doing it. Opium was very popular in China. Someone came over to us in the den and offered us a job we couldn't turn down. We had to travel by sewer, climb up into the palace and kill the Emperor. Jenkies never made it out of the sewer."

A sense of déjà vu trickles over the nurses as they realise it's just another made-up story and they haven't made any progress at all.

"Me and Flic made it to the Emperor, but once I killed him, all these ninjas turned up out of nowhere. That was a struggle, but thankfully we'd had some karate lessons previously and so we managed to be on a par with them. I killed the last one, and looked round for Flic. She was hurt. Sliced right down the middle, but she was still alive... For a moment. All I got to say was 'goodbye' before she passed away from her injuries..."

Len flops sullenly back down in his chair after his performance. Nobody speaks for a while, unsure about what they can say to him.

"This meeting is over." Atilla stands and exits the room without saying anything more.

Adesso takes Mr Lewis' restraint off and he follows the rest of the nurses into the staffroom. The patients, left to their own devices, slowly leave the room themselves.

Mr Lewis walks over to Len and takes his hands in his. "Thank you for protecting me, Len. Everyone here is too scared to help anymore." As he says this, he unknowingly shakes Len's hand about a hundred times, but he doesn't mind.

"It's not fair." Len shakes his head, feeling genuine sympathy for the old man.

"And between you and me... I love your stories! Very thrilling!" He jumps excitedly, letting go of Len and wandering down the stairwell to the dayroom.

Meanwhile, in the staffroom...

"What are we gonna do? I need this cash reward!" Adesso shouts in frustration.

"We need to know what makes him tick." Atilla rubs her hairy chin.

"His girlfriend?" Paul puts his hand up before he answers.

"Shush Paul, we're trying to –" She stops herself, thinking about what he said. "You're right!"

That's the first time Paul has been praised by her. They all look around at each other, smirking. They've got him now.

CHAPTER FIVE

B y the time Len makes it to the dayroom, the single game of poker allowed for the day is already in motion. He walks straight over, ignoring anything else in the room. It's the usual players, The Dealer, Big Al, Scott Green and Theo – but this time, Eucalyptus and DJ Gurns are there too.

"Morning, Len." Big Al smiles brightly, in contrast to the grey rain hitting the windows behind her.

"Good morning. I can't believe I missed the next game." He holds his hand out to reference the poker table.

"You might as well take DJ's place, he's been staring like that since the first hand," Theo moans, rolling his eyes.

Len looks around the table, unsure about whether he should. He eyeballs DJ Gurns, who sits slumped back onto his wooden chair. His eyes look like they are practically in the back of his head under his low eyelids, and his overalls are rolled down to his waist displaying his clean white t-shirt despite a few dribble patches.

"Go on," Big Al nods to a chair, "just pull that chair up behind him."

He does, but also decides to take it a step further. Without anyone noticing, he pulls DJ's arms out of his sleeves and puts his own arms in them instead, and picks up the two, as of yet, unseen cards in front of him.

"Al right guys, last card... Ten of hearts." The Dealer flips the card into the line with the rest.

Yeeeees, we've got a flush, DJ!

"Eucalyptus?" The Dealer waits for her response,

"All in." She smiles as she pushes her cigarettes into the middle.

She's bluffing.

"DJ?"

"All in!" Len says, throwing his cards onto the table, continuing to throw cigarettes one by one into the middle of the table with his arms in DJ's sleeves.

Everyone laughs, sparking Len to do more dramatic things with his arms, scratching DJ's nipple and picking his nose.

"Big Al?" The Dealer says, trying not to laugh.

"I'll call as well," she says, as she wipes a tear from below her eye.

"All right, show us what you've got."

Eucalyptus turns her cards over; four of clubs and nine of diamonds... nothing.

"Ehhh... So, Eucalyptus has nothing," the Dealer narrates.

"*WHAT? NOTHING?*" she screams suddenly, making everybody jump. Her face has morphed from sweet and down-to-earth, to looking like a bull with a bee in its mouth.

"Do you even know how to play poker?" Theo shakes his head. "Who let her play?"

She storms over to him and flips his chair backwards. He lands on the floor with a crack. She looks like she's about to punch him when she spins around rapidly and smiles again.

"Shall we have a game of poker?" She looks at all the strained faces around the table.

The crowd has now disappeared and it's only the players left.

"We're just winding it down now, mate. We'll have another game tomorrow." Big Al smiles and nods at her.

"Okay!" She shrugs her shoulders up to her chin and smiles again, walking away.

Theo picks himself up off the floor, leaving the broken chair where it is and sitting on another one.

"So much for nurses protecting us," Theo spits through gritted teeth, resentment for both the nurses and Eucalyptus coming through.

"Shall we finish the game? You might as well turn them over together," The Dealer instructs.

Big Al and Len flip their cards over at the same time.

"Flush!" they both announce.

They look each other over before leaning across the table to see who has the higher card.

Len has the ace of hearts, Al's highest being the Jack of hearts.

"Wooo!" Len cheers, spinning his arms, that are still in the sleeves, around DJ's head.

Everyone laughs again, and he takes his arms out and replaces them with DJ's once again.

"Here's your winnings." The Dealer pushes them over to Len.

"I think I'll let DJ keep them." Len pats him on the shoulder as he stands up from his chair.

Suddenly, DJ grabs the pile of winnings in his hand and throws them all behind his shoulder, his face still in the same gormless stare. He comes out of his trance and looks around. "Who won?"

"You, mate." Scott laughs. "Your winnings are on the floor behind you."

He jumps up out of the chair and scrambles on the floor, nearly knocking Len over on his way down.

Big Al gets up from the table, followed by Scott and Theo.

"Shall we go for a smoke?" she asks the three of them.

"Obviously!" Scott celebrates.

They leave DJ and The Dealer to pack away the cards as they head for the secret door in the kitchen.

Cookie isn't visible in the kitchen today, so they go straight up without staying to chat. When they finally get there, they find the four chairs positioned close together under a big umbrella with a beer logo imprinted across the cover, and they quickly run through the rain to congregate under it.

Scott takes a spliff out of the cig packet in his pocket again and lights it, blowing a lungful of smoke onto the burning end.

"C-can I ask you guys a question?" Len stutters, not sure if he really wants to know the answer.

"Sure," they all reply.

"Why are you in here? You all seem somewhat normal," he states.

"*Somewhat?*" Big Al laughs as she takes the spliff from in between Scott's slender fingers.

"You know what I mean." Len rubs his neck, still feeling the pain from the headboard.

"Delirium. Too many drugs fucked up my brain," Scott explains, flicking his mullet from his shoulder.

"Depression and self-harm. My dad died when I was young, and my crackhead mum got me sent to the dumping ground. It all went downhill from there." Theo pouts and shrugs his mental illnesses away.

"And you, Al?" Len mutters; this is the one he was scared about.

"Erm... I'd rather not say." She twiddles her fingers on her knee and passes the spliff to Theo. "I'm all about mystery." She winks, pulling herself back together.

"What about you, Len? Are those stories you tell everybody true?" Theo asks.

Len thinks about his answer before he speaks. "Honestly... No." He hangs his head.

"Can't deal with the truth just yet?" Scott nods his head a few times in agreement with his own statement.

"I guess you could say that, yeah." Len brings his head up again to take the joint from Theo.

"Don't worry, you don't have to tell us... yet." Theo smirks at him.

"Some of it is true. I suppose I just don't want to tell that horrible nurse. I feel like they're trying to trick me," Len explains as he takes a drag.

Big Al nods her head glumly.

"I know what you mean, mate." Scott pats Len gently on the shoulder for comfort.

They head back downstairs and into the food hall, where nurses have set the tables up for lunch as usual.

"Hey, Ace." Adesso runs over to the group.

"Hi, what's up?" Al asks him.

"Just wanted to let you know we've got a game on tonight at eight," he whispers, hoping the others don't hear.

They do.

"Sound, I'll be there." She smiles at him and starts to walk away; the others trail behind.

"What's he on about?" Len whispers to Theo.

"Poker," he whispers back.

A heavy hand lands on both of their shoulders, as if their shadows had finally had enough of following them around.

"It's rude to whisper, boys." Adesso leans his intimidating face in between theirs.

They continue looking forward in fright.

"Yes, sir," Theo splutters and runs off to join Al and Scott by the door.

Adesso spins Len around to face him. He towers over Len by at least a foot. "I'm gonna get to the bottom of you, boy." He glares down at Len.

Len backs away slowly before turning around to leave. As he does so, Adesso slaps him on the arse. Len looks at him over his shoulder and Adesso throws his head back, pushing a hearty laugh out between his perfect teeth.

"Take no notice of him, Len," Big Al tells him.

She allows everyone to pass her before she and Adesso lock eyes across the room, him still smiling, Big Al not so impressed. She says nothing and goes back into the dayroom.

CHAPTER SIX

F or the first time in years, a verbal announcement is sent through the speakers about a full group meeting for the patients. Only the ones that aren't allowed in the dayroom are exempt.

Everyone gathers around. The circle structure wouldn't work for this many people and so it's set out like a stage, with a big audience of crazy people, Eucalyptus, Al, Len, Scott and Theo on the front row. The nurses hang around on stage, waiting for the star of the show. Paul is fidgeting and stepping from one foot to another, looking at Len. He finally has enough courage to go over.

"Hi, Len. It's me, Paul." He bends down to level with Len's eyes.

"Hi, Paul." Len gives a slight smile.

"I was wondering... First of all, if you'll sign my book," he passes his copy of *Gone Too Far West* to Len, "and secondly... Can you get me into the next book? I'll buy a million copies!" He giggles nervously.

"I don't have a pen... and I don't write books," Len replies.

Paul passes him a pen from his breast pocket and waits patiently for him to sign it.

"What do you want me to write?" Len asks.

"Erm... 'To Paul, you're the best nurse in town. Love from your friend, Len'... Please." He beams.

He peers over the lip of the book to watch Len write his well-thought-out message on the inside cover page.

Atilla bursts through the double doors and Paul snatches the book off Len, whispers his thank-you and scuttles back with the rest of the nurses. Len puts the pen in his pocket.

Atilla takes centre stage; the spotlight is only on her.

"Hello, everyone. This is something that we've never done before, but we thought it would be a nice surprise for you all," she begins.

A projector is rolled into the room by Adesso, and he sets it up behind the audience. Like at the cinema, the beam of light illuminates the space above their heads, uncovering the cloud of dust swirling around the room.

"We contacted your families yesterday, and asked them to send us some pictures in... Of you, and your loved ones." She looks at Len. "Let's see who we've got first."

A black and white picture of a young boy sitting on the knee of his mother, a beautiful woman with thick hair pulled atop of her head in a loose bun. Her husband stands formally behind her with a hand on her shoulder, dressed in his best suit. On the other side of her, another young boy stands grumpily with his arms tightly folded across his chest; the face is slightly familiar.

"Mother." Mr Lewis' voice shakes as he says it.

Eucalyptus turns around to him and says, "Look at you, Mr Lewis! Cute as a button!"

Before he has time to reminisce, the next picture flickers onto the wall. It's a picture of Scott, standing between two of his friends. They have their arms around each other and their glassy eyes look straight past the camera.

"Good night?" Al laughs and hits Scott on the leg.

"You know it, mate!" He laughs, too and begins to think about how many drugs he actually took that night.

The next picture on the wall is of a young girl wearing loose-fitting dungarees with nothing on underneath. She's sitting in the middle of a fresh green field on a perfect summer's day, and in her arms is a tiny lamb that she feeds through a bottle.

"Awww, I loved that baby, I called her Ophelia," Eucalyptus sings, holding her clasped hands under her chin.

"Nice name..." Theo says sarcastically, but quietly enough for her not to hear him.

Next up is a picture of Theo in the orphanage. He has thick braces poking out of his mouth and his chino shorts are pulled up to his neck, secured with a belt.

"What fucking neck size are them shorts, Theo?" Scott howls.

Only the front row is laughing hysterically, apart from Theo who has slid down into his chair in a strop.

Pictures of the other patients are quickly flashed up onto the wall, and then it's Len's turn.

"Last but *certainly* not least," Atilla introduces the final picture.

It's one of Len with his three best friends, Jav, Jenkies and Flic. It's a picture from the happiest moment of their lives, the day they did shrooms in Amsterdam. Flic is at the front, taking the picture, Len behind her and Jenkies behind him, and Javan is lower down on the bed, leaning in. They're all smiles, looking like the best of friends.

The picture seems to be left on longer than any of the others. Nobody comments on this one, but all eyes are on Len.

29

His eyes are on nothing but the picture. He's not seen it in ages; he misses their faces.

Without saying anything he begins to bite his nails.

"What do you think, Len?" Atilla asks smugly.

"I think..." he replies, unblinking, "I think... I look really good in that picture." He nods gently to himself.

Big Al covers her grin with her overalls. He's always one step ahead.

"And what about your girlfriend?" Atilla asks again, sounding slightly more cross this time.

"Yeah, she's alright. Not as good as me, though. Wouldn't you agree?" He smiles at Atilla this time.

"I don't know if 'good' is a word you can use to describe a murderer, Len." She strides closer to him. "I don't know whether you killed him, or your little girlfriend did it, so to me, both of you are just as evil as each other." She glares directly into his eyes.

He stands up and gets right in her face. "Don't you DARE speak about Flic like that!" He punches Atilla square in the nose and she's knocked flat on the floor. The patients cheer and carry Len on their shoulders chanting his name. At least that's what happened in his head, anyway. "Okay," he replies mildly, containing his rage.

"Is that it, 'okay'?" Atilla spits.

"Yep."

Atilla straightens up but doesn't take her eyes off of Len. She can see the anger inside of him. Now she knows that talking about Flic works, they'll get it all out of him in no time. "I think we should have a one-to-one, don't you, Len?" she says.

"Like a date?" he asks. The room fills with hushed giggles.

Atilla smiles to appease them. "Sure, it's a date."

He smiles. "What time shall I pick you up?"

"Why don't we just go now?" She begins to grow impatient.

"But Mrs Hunning, we hardly know each other!"

"Then let's get to know each other." She grabs Len by the arm and drags him out of his seat.

Wolf-whistles arise from the audience. "Have her back by seven!" someone shouts.

She ignores them and exits the room without looking back, Len's arm still tightly clasped in her gorilla hand. Before they disappear through the doors, Len glances back at Al. She's already looking at him with a worried face, but she throws him a quick thumbs-up before he's on his own.

Atilla's office is very stark. No pictures of family or friends; no pictures at all, in fact. The walls are beige and covered only in lists of names or other formal pieces of paper. The only noise in the room is the low hum of the air-conditioning. The chair he sits on is wooden and falling apart, but the dirty grey suede backrest is regrettably comfortable.

Atilla's perch is more of a throne than a chair. It has every amenity one could need, except a cup holder. Behind her is a certificate:

Doctor of Psychology, proudly presented to Bertha Hunning.

"Bertha... You suit that name." Len smiles, to appear polite.

"Well, now we know each other's names, we can get down to business," she says, her face stiff as a board.

"This is moving a little too quickly for me, Bertha." Len holds his hands up.

"I'd prefer if you continued to call me Mrs Hunning."

"Whatever you want." Len smiles.

"What I want, Mr Moscow, is to know whether or not you murdered that man. There is no need for you to be in here if you didn't do it."

There'd be no need for him to be in here if he said yes, either. He'd be sent straight to prison for life.

"Why does everyone suddenly think it was me? You read the book, didn't you? Flic admitted to it!"

"Yes, but there's one problem, Len. She's dead. And everyone agrees that you've been acting strange recently, giving us all a valid excuse to suspect you. Now, you can either tell us the truth, or you can be stuck in here forever," she lectures him.

He thinks about it, his eyes darting back and forth along the floor as if a mini tennis match was being played below him. He thinks about his family, his future, what will happen to him if he doesn't tell the truth. He takes a deep breath.

"What do you want to know?"

The dayroom is back to its usual layout by the time Len solemnly returns, dragging his feet along the floor. He notices his friends sitting watching the door, awaiting his return. They all run up to him.

"Len, what did she do to you?" Theo desperately grabs onto Len's arm.

"She said if I don't tell the truth, I'll never leave this place." He scans their faces.

"So... What did you tell her?" Big Al asks him.

"I told her about the time when we all went to the Sea Kingdom and killed the mermaid queen." He laughs.

They all laugh in relief,

"Bet she didn't take that well," Scott says.

"She didn't... I've got another meeting tomorrow. She told me to sleep on it, rethink my answer," he explains.

"What are you going to do?" Al quizzes.

"I don't know yet..."

"At least you're safe for now." Theo pats him on the back.

"Yeah, for now." Len's head is full of worries.

Bedtime arrives at the hospital. The corridors seem eerier than usual, not a sound to be heard other than light snores and the odd scream from a night terror. Len lies on his back, eyes open, staring into the darkness. For a long time, he thinks about nothing, just stares. He hears the distant sound of a door opening, one of the heavy cell doors that lock the patients into their rooms. He slowly gets out of bed and pushes his head as far out of the barred window as possible, to see down the corridor. No movement. He tries the handle of his own door; no movement again.

He looks at the digital clock that's screwed onto the wall: 8:10pm

He hears the stairwell door open at the end of the corridor,

"Al?" he whispers loudly.

No reply.

"What ye doin, bru?" He hears the whisper right down his ear.

He jumps and spins around to find Mehzah's silhouette directly in front of him, the light from the window only slightly illuminating the curves of his face.

Len lets out a huge breath of relief and laughs while he rubs his eyes with his thumb and index finger.

"Sorry. Did I wake you up?" he asks Mehzah.

"I never sleep," he whispers.

"Oh, right..." Len pushes past him and sits on his bed, his bare feet growing colder on the icy floor.

Mehzah sits across from Len on his own bed and stares at him through the darkness.

"What were you going to tell me about Al?" Len asks, remembering their conversation from this morning.

"I hear everything around here, bru. It's easy to sneak around when nobody notices ye," Mehzah explains.

"So, what have you heard?"

Mehzah lies back down onto his creaky bed.

"All I'm saying is, stay away from her," he whispers again.

"Why?"

"Ye can find that out for yeself, if ye really want to."

CHAPTER SEVEN

The patients follow orders from the alarms: wake up, shower, dress, now sit around and do nothing.

But not all the patients.

Big Al, Theo, Scott and Len are all sitting in the secret dining room in the kitchen, at 8am sharp. They are trying to come up with a plausible story for Len to tell Atilla in just one hour.

"Right, we'll have no mention of pirates, Chinamen or mermaids in this one, thank you, Len." Scott laughs.

"Can't promise anything," Len joins in, smiling.

"Let's plan it out. Does anyone have a pen?" Big Al asks.

"Yeah," Len begins, digging into his pocket.

"Why don't you just tell the truth, Len?" Theo breaks the light-hearted atmosphere.

Everyone goes quiet and looks at Theo and then to Len.

After what seems like forever, he finally opens his mouth. "I don't know..." He looks glumly at the table.

Nobody knows what to say and the awkwardness of the

situation starts to prickle into their skin as they become more and more aware of the silence enclosing them in together.

"Len and I are going for a walk," Big Al declares as she stands up from the table.

They look up at her, all slightly relieved to have been saved from this moment of unease. Len stands up to join her and they exit the room, leaving Scott and Theo alone together.

"What do you think about Len?" Theo asks him.

"He's sound," Scott replies.

"Do you reckon he actually killed someone?"

"I don't know. He says he didn't, so that's what I believe."

"Why doesn't he tell the truth then? There's more to his stories than he's letting on."

"Don't go digging, Theo. He's supposed to be our friend," Scott says, getting slightly agitated now.

He gets up from the table and walks out of the room without a second glance at Theo, who is now sulking with his head leaning hard against the table.

Big Al leads Len into the staff corridor. "Wait here," she whispers, with her finger on her lips.

Len mimics her by putting his finger to his lips, too, leaning up against the wall.

Al knocks the usual 'shave and a haircut – two bits', on the window of the staffroom door before opening it herself and striding in.

"What's up, Ace?" Len hears someone say before the door completely shuts.

He leans in closer to hear, putting his ear on the crack of the door.

"Keys... walk... beautiful day... fresh air..."

Nothing interesting, Len thinks to himself. He straightens up again, now that he's not bothered about listening in.

Al strolls back out a few seconds later, smiling and swinging a pair of keys around her finger. "Let's go."

They walk down the corridor and she unlocks a grey door that has the same bars on it as all the other windows and doors in the facility, only this one opens out onto the grounds of the hospital, full of luscious green grass and tall trees of oak and beech.

"Why do the nurses treat you so well compared to everyone else?" Len asks.

"I've known them for a long time. I help them out when they need it and they help me," she explains as she locks the door behind them.

"Help them how?"

She turns her back to the door and looks Len steadily in the eyes. "However they need," she says, before gliding past him and beginning their route through the grounds.

The gravel crunches under their shoes as they stroll along the path. Al takes a deep lungful of crisp air and scans everything she can see around her, looking up into the foliage of the trees, hoping to spot a bird or a squirrel, and scanning the floor for any signs of life.

"How long have you been in here for, then?" Len breaks the peaceful silence.

"Too long." She laughs.

Len shoves his hands into his pockets, his shoulders rising up to his jaw out of nervousness.

"Shall we sit on this bench here?" Al points to an old wooden bench covered in moss.

"If it's the only bench," Len scoffs.

"It is." She smiles at him.

They perch on the bench, attempting to dodge the moss and bird shit that covers it.

"Len, I need to tell you something..." she begins.

"What?" he answers quickly, hoping it's something to do with her and why she's the bad person Mehzah made her out to be.

"It's about your stories," she begins. Len's interest drops slightly. "People are going to get bored with it. The nurses already are. But if you lose your alliance with the patients, too, you're screwed."

Len says nothing. Al looks him over, waiting for a reply. Once she realises there won't be one, she continues. "What is the true story, Len? Someone needs to know."

"People *do* know, it's all in the book. I just can't bring myself to say that Flic did what she did." Len hangs his head, his shoulder blades almost touching behind him.

"But Len... If you didn't do anything wrong, you shouldn't be in here!"

"Maybe I want to be in here." He tilts his head up to look her in the eyes.

"Why would you want to be here?" she puzzles, visibly.

"I have no life out there anymore... At least I have you guys in here." He places his hand on her knee and squeezes it gently.

She blushes guiltily and puts her hand on his,

"You can't stay here forever, Len..." She checks the time on her watch. "You've got your meeting with Atilla in fifteen minutes, we should head back."

He nods and they get up off the bench and head back to the dreary old building.

"What are you going to tell her, then?" Al asks.

"I haven't figured it out yet," he replies, still staring at the ground.

"Well... I hope you make the right decision, Len." She smiles weakly to herself.

They make it back to the staffroom for Al to give the keys back just in time, as Atilla comes out of the room after her.

"Shall we go to my office, Len?" she says plainly.

"Yeah..." He nods, looking at Al, who, in front of Atilla, looks like David losing his battle against Goliath.

She throws him a worried-looking smile before they go their opposite ways down the hall.

Once they sit down on opposing sides of the desk, Atilla moves straight in for the attack. "So... No more messing around. Tell me what happened, Len."

He takes a deep breath and thinks about his answer. "All right. We were in Paradox Park, taking shrooms for the first time, smoking some other stuff as well."

"What stuff?" Atilla interrupts, as she writes down the important parts of the story.

"Weed."

She nods for him to continue.

"And we were just waiting to come up when... this shadow appears."

"Gaz?" she interrupts again.

"Yeah. We were all scared to death of him. I honestly thought I was going to die that night. But then he left, after smoking some of our weed."

"Where did he go?"

"Into the forest behind us. That was the last time I saw him."

Atilla raises a suspicious eyebrow but writes it down anyway.

39

"Then the drugs start to kick in, and that's when it got weird."

"Why?" she asks.

"I was the captain of a ship, Jenkies, Jav and Flic were my crew – and..."

"Oh, shut up, Len. We've heard this pirate bullshit before! Just tell the truth!" Atilla bellows.

"That *is* the truth! I was hallucinating!" he shouts back.

"Hallucinations are *not* the truth." She scowls at him, now leaning over the table. Len wonders how her wrists are holding that much weight.

"Fine." He frowns, standing up to level with Atilla's eyes. "Then I don't know the truth."

She straightens, flaring her nostrils as if there's a bad smell in the room,

"Get out." She says it softly, but the anger inside her is apparent.

They stare each other down for another moment or two before Len quickly leaves the room, half slamming the door behind him.

Atilla suddenly lets out the breath of air she'd been holding back in her lungs as she flops down into her chair. She wonders if they'll ever get to the bottom of this case. If he was telling the truth, everyone will think she is as crazy as he is for believing such nonsense. But she knows he was telling the truth for once; they just need to find a way to make it sound plausible.

There wasn't much left that Len could do; he'd tried to tell the truth and that ended up getting him into even more trouble. As he storms down the corridor, the first traces of tears beginning to swell and sting in his eyes, he thinks only of one thing: from now on, he's doing things his own way.

CHAPTER EIGHT

Instead of returning to the dayroom like he usually would, Len sneaks his way back up to his room on the second floor, in order to construct a plan of action. No more listening to other people's advice, he thinks: only he can help himself.

He sits down on his hard mattress, his head in his hands, trying to think of a plan. He picks up one of Mehzah's comics and flicks through the pages, trying to find one with enough blank space for him to write his plan on. He finds one towards the back of the comic and pulls out the pen in his pocket. He scribbles furiously on the page, so he doesn't miss a single idea that's swelling up and out of his mind.

He jabs the page with the pen to mark a victorious full stop and then puts the pen back into his pocket before reading back over his plan with feverish excitement.

"What are you doing up here?" Randall interrupts from the doorway.

Len jumps into action, but thinks better of hiding the comic book from Randall, knowing what he's like,

"Just reading this comic," he replies, innocently flicking through the pages again.

"You're usually downstairs with Big Al and the gang." He readies his notepad.

"I feel like being on my own right now."

Randall begins to write down Len's response but once he interprets it in his head, he stops. "Okay. I'll leave you," he says and turns away.

"Wait!" Len stops him. "What do you write down in there?"

"Any dirt I can dig up on the patients," he replies frankly, turning around to face Len again.

"Why?"

"So I stay on the nurses' good side," he explains, inching further into Len's room.

Len ponders this for a moment. "So... do you have stuff on every patient?" He glances expectantly at Randall.

"Who do you wanna know about?" Randall smirks, sitting down on Mehzah's bed across from Len.

"Big Al?" Len hesitates.

"Big Al... Big Al..." Randall repeats as he licks his finger and flips the pages over. "*Heeeere* we go..."

Len edges closer to Randall, the adrenaline pumping through him now.

"Len, there you are. We've been looking everywhere for you," Big Al says worriedly from the doorway.

Both Len and Randall jump out of their skin once they see whose mouth those words had travelled from. Randall flips his notebook closed and stands, shaking like a shitting dog.

"What's he doing here?" Theo spits, trying to push in between Al and Scott in the doorway.

"He was trying to dig up some dirt on me, weren't you Randall?" Len says, giving him hints with his eyes.

"Uh, yeah. But I've decided against it now. I won't bother any of you again if you just let me live!" Randall pleads.

Big Al pushes out a laugh between her lips and looks at Scott and Theo, who are smirking too. She smiles kindly at Randall and steps into the room, out of the doorway, giving him a clear path to freedom. He scuttles towards it straight away, but Scott is there to block him at the last minute,

"I don't want to see you talking to Len again, all right?" he whispers to him.

Randall nods violently in agreement and Scott pats him on the back, letting him go. He runs straight to the staffroom.

Al takes up Randall's old seat on Mehzah's bed and crosses her leg over the other, staring straight at Len. He can feel the conviction wrap around him like a cape.

"What happened in the meeting?" she finally asks.

"She didn't believe me," he replies.

"Oh, Len," Al sympathises, putting her hand on his knee.

He leans back slightly and his hand brushes over the open comic book sprawled out on the bed next to him. He quickly tries to think of a way to hide it without anyone noticing. He begins to slowly push it under his pillow.

Theo and Scott come to join them after disposing of Randall. Theo pushes past Al's arm and plonks down next to Len, sitting directly on the comic.

"Oops, what's this?" He laughs, pulling it out from under his bum.

"Ehh, it's just one of Mehzah's comics, I was flicking through it." He scrambles, trying to get it out of Theo's hands as soon as possible.

"*The Adventures of Sewer Boy*. What a weirdo!" He laughs again, scanning over the cover and the inside pages.

"Yeah. Haha... Look at this," Len says, taking the comic

from Theo and looking for a page with something notable to show them.

"DISPERSE!" A loud voice booms through the stark room.

It's Atilla. They all look over at her and then each other, before standing up and exiting the room silently. Len takes this opportunity to shove the comic under his pillow at last.

Atilla eyeballs Len as he squeezes past her but says nothing to him.

The lunchtime alarm rings and the patients file into the food hall.

Len, who hasn't said a word since being kicked out of his room, pulls up a seat next to Mr Lewis on the long communal table. Al, Scott and Theo wander past on their way to the secret dining room and spot him seated there with everyone else.

"Hey, Len. Aren't you coming with us?" Theo shouts over.

"Think I'm gonna stay here," he replies quietly.

Al looks at Len for a long time before she continues on her path to the kitchen, shortly followed by the other two.

Although it was what he wanted to do, Len feels terrible about ditching his new friends for a bit of alone time. He needs to think about what he's going to do.

Mr Lewis leans over and smiles at him. "Tell me another one of your stories, Len."

"I don't have any more stories, Mr Lewis."

"Of course you do, boy! You're a great storyteller!" he praises.

Len, equipped with this new ego boost, smirks and begins to appease old Mr Lewis.

"Well... I do have *one* other story." He blushes.

Mr Lewis tucks his napkin into the neck of his t-shirt and gets comfy with his plate, ready to listen.

"It was 1969 and countries all over the world were fighting to be the first to have astronauts land on the moon!"

"Impossible!" Mr Lewis smiles like an excited child.

"That's what everybody thought, but do you know who succeeded? Not Russia. Not America. England! Because I was the head astronaut of a fleet of Brainiacs called Felicity, Jenkinson and Javan. Together, we successfully pulled off a full orbit around the earth, then the moon, and then we landed safely in a moon crater."

"Extraordinary." Mr Lewis shakes his head.

"I'll tell you what was extraordinary – the aliens! They were long, about nine feet tall, they were green, like weed, and the drugs they supplied us... huhuhuh, that was NOT like weed! When we first landed, they were scared of us, they thought humans weren't clever enough to ever land on the moon, so when we landed, they thought we must be some sort of unbelievable being... and of course I was. We earned their trust and they took us to the alien leader, whose name was General Gleck. His palace was something else! He showed us around, and the last stop was his partying room, full of hookahs and possible hookers. He forced us to smoke it, really, but we didn't put up that much of a fight. It was like LSD times a thousand! Everything was swirling and pulsing and sounds were distorted, too, colours were constantly changing. At one point, Javan started to get really anxious, saying he thought General Gleck had drugged us to make us easier to exterminate. So, in our drugged-up haze, we tried to kill him. I'm pretty sure I managed to hit him over the head hard enough and we ran back to the rocket and made it back to earth safely."

"Wow! Incredible story, Len!" Mr Lewis finishes his meal and starts to clap quickly.

Len grins smugly and puts his hand up for him to stop, even though he wants it to go on forever. "Please. Please. That's enough." He smirks.

A slow, loud clap begins to drown out Mr Lewis', and Len looks around to see who his other admirer is.

"Yeeeeah, cute story, Len," Adesso mocks, getting closer to Len with each clap. "It's just a shame that you can't seem to tell the truth."

"Who cares if he's telling the truth?" Mr Lewis stands up from his chair, waving his fist at Adesso. "His stories are good!"

"Sit down, Mr Lewis. The only reason he's here is because of his lies."

"They're not lies, they're stories!" he shouts louder, and steps even closer to Adesso.

"I won't tell you again, Mr Lewis. Sit down, or I'll be forced to take you downstairs."

"You leave the boy alone! He's traumatised, don't you see?" Mr Lewis grabs hold of Adesso's arms and shakes him.

"That's it." He takes the whistle dangling from his pocket and blows it three times, "You're coming with us, we need to teach you how to behave." He takes a tight grip of Mr Lewis' arms and pulls them behind him.

"No! You can't do this! I don't deserve it!" Mr Lewis cries, as five other nurses arrive to help restrain him.

They circle him and forcefully attach Mr Lewis to the ironing board like Hannibal Lecter, as if he were in the same category.

None of the patients have enough courage to speak up at this point, but Al, Theo and Scott have emerged from out of the kitchen to witness the commotion.

The nurses begin to wheel him towards the doors.

"Never stop telling your story, Len! FREEDOM!

FREEDOM!" He screams like a madman until he can no longer be heard.

The food hall is suddenly deadly silent and all eyes are on Len. He looks around nervously at everyone. They think he's to blame, or he didn't do enough to save Mr Lewis after he just stood up for him.

Al is leaning on the kitchen counter with her hands over her mouth. She knows there's nothing to do for Mr Lewis now, but there's still hope for Len yet.

She walks over without saying anything and gives Len a hug around the neck, her cheek leaning on top of his head. He holds onto her arms and nuzzles his head against them, closing his eyes.

"Don't worry, Len," she says to him, stroking his head lightly with her cheek.

"What's downstairs?" His voice cracks.

Al pulls away and looks down at his worried face. "It's not good..." She sighs.

"You have to save him, Al," he pleads, snatching her hand into his.

"There's nothing that I can do –"

"There's always something *you* can do!"

Shocked, she steps back, letting her hand fall out of Len's grasp.

"Please, Al."

She doesn't reply for a long time, thinking about what she could actually do to help.

"I can't do anything for him right now... But once he comes back up, I know what we can do." She nods.

Len stands up and gives her a tight hug,

"Thanks, Al," he says and gives her a big kiss on the cheek.

CHAPTER NINE

"Here's the plan," Al begins, spreading the blueprints of the hospital across the secret dining room table. "The staffroom is here, and the room where they keep all the drugs is here." She points to rooms across from each other.

"What drug do we need?" Scott asks. It is his specialist subject, after all.

"It's called Ambien, it helps activate dormant brain cells. It should be in a white bottle," she explains.

"Whereabouts will it be?" Len asks.

"I'm not sure. We'll just need to look around." She rubs her finger over her bottom lip, thinking. "We need one person to distract any nurses that we need to get rid of, one person as lookout outside the door, one person to get the key from the staffroom and get the Ambien, and one person to give it to Mr Lewis. So, who wants to do what?"

"I think you're the only one who has a chance of getting the key," Len says to Al.

"You're probably right," she agrees.

"I'll be lookout," Theo volunteers.

"I'll give the drug to Mr Lewis," Scott volunteers next.

"Looks like you have the job of distracting the nurses then, Len," Al says.

"That shouldn't be a problem." He smiles.

With the plan singed into their brain, they make their way into the dayroom, awaiting Mr Lewis' return.

Despite waiting all evening for any sign of Mr Lewis, he did not appear. Their plan is on hold until the time is right.

That time comes the next day after lunch. Everyone is in the dayroom going about their usual business. Apart from the four of them, all the other patients have already forgotten about what happened to Mr Lewis the previous afternoon. That is, until he is wheeled back into the dayroom by Adesso. He props the wheelchair up against the wall and puts the brakes on. He looks around at the patients who are now all staring at him, frozen in fear.

"Let this be a warning to you all!" he shouts to everyone, and leaves the room.

Mr Lewis hasn't blinked or moved an inch since being left there. Al and Len walk over to him; Theo and Scott stay away in order to look inconspicuous. They bend down to his level on either side of him and they put a hand on each of his.

"Are you okay, Mr Lewis?" Len asks him.

No reply.

"Can you hear us?" Al asks.

No reply.

They look at each other and then back to the lifeless old man.

"Don't worry, we're gonna make you better again soon," Al whispers to him and pats him on the hand.

They stand up to regroup with Theo and Scott. Al looks down the corridor as she turns around to leave and spots Adesso talking to Atilla right outside the staffroom.

"Okay, guys. Atilla and Adesso are in the corridor so, Len, you need to do something to get the attention of both of them and get them out of there before we can do anything."

"I've got an idea." He begins to laugh. "Wait there." He walks off behind the wall that separates the dayroom and the food hall.

The three of them stare at the wall, waiting to see what his brilliant idea is. Suddenly, a naked Len runs through the dayroom and towards the corridor, his hand being his only cover.

"GO, GO, GO!" he shouts, with a big smile on his face.

The three of them burst into astonished laughter, prompting the other patients to look. Eucalyptus catches a glimpse of his white buttocks running towards the door and she decides to join in.

"WOOHOO!" she sings, stripping off and following Len down the corridor.

Al, Scott and Theo barely regain their composure as they pace towards the staffroom themselves. Al quickly ducks into the staffroom and scans the cabinet full of keys. There are a couple that have a label saying *Medicine Room*, and so she takes both of them and rushes back into the corridor.

Theo is already standing guard opposite the staffroom, with Scott waiting at the double doors entering the dayroom, ready to give the drug to Mr Lewis as soon as.

Al tries the first key, but although it fits, it doesn't turn in the lock. She tries the other key and this time it unlocks the door with a satisfying click. She hurriedly enters the small room, shuts the door behind her and begins to scour the cupboards for the Ambien. Above her, she can hear the running footsteps of Len and the closely following angry mob he's picked up along the way. She laughs to herself and scans the labels on the white bottles. She finally finds the one that says *AMBIEN* on the bottom shelf and in one swift movement she unscrews the lid, tips a pill into her hand and screws the lid back on.

She reaches for the handle and opens the door slightly, but it's dragged shut again just as quickly. She stands frozen in the dark room, waiting and listening.

She hears Paul's voice. "What's going on here? Where are all the nurses?"

"They're running after Len. They need your help. First floor!" Theo shouts urgently, sparking Paul to run down the corridor.

The door swings open again and Al steps out, looking both ways across the corridor. She sees Paul running away on the other side and Scott waiting eagerly near the dayroom. Al mimics a basketball shot to let Scott know she's going to throw it, and he preps himself, bending the knees and making a W with his hands. The long, white pill flies through the air towards Scott. Before it even arrives in his hands, Al is back in the staffroom to return the keys safely.

Scott makes the catch and manages to shove it into Mr Lewis' mouth and make him drink, just in time before Adesso and Atilla arrive back into the corridor with Len and Eucalyptus draped in blankets.

Len looks up and spots the three of them looking smugly at him from the dayroom. He smiles at them and they begin to clap for him. Soon enough, even patients who don't have a clue what's going on are clapping as well.

"Stop that! That spectacle is nothing to applaud!" Atilla screams, letting her anger show through for the first time since anyone can remember.

Len comes closer to get a better look at everyone clapping for him; just behind Atilla's steaming face, he's laughing. Astonishingly, still unable to control his face, Mr Lewis manages to heave up his heavy hands and gently clap for his hero and saviour, Len.

CHAPTER TEN

F riday arrives at the hospital. Whilst most people are excited and eager to celebrate the weekend ahead, our patients notice no difference; every day is just as miserable as the one before. The only ray of light being Mr Lewis' quick recovery. He's still in his wheelchair, but now he can talk and move his arms, which is all he really needs, anyway.

Mr Lewis has been given a new outlook on life, thanks to Len. He could have been in that state for the rest of his life, but now that he's been brought back from the dead, he has no intentions of returning. He sits contentedly humming old wartime tunes over the top of the unmelodic beats being spat out of DJ's mouth.

The gang are sat across the room, playing their usual game of midday poker. They're all guilty of taking quick glances at Mr Lewis, just to check if he's okay.

"It's nice to see him back to his happy self." Al smiles, looking lovingly at Mr Lewis.

Len swivels his head round to see him.

"Yeah, he's such a great guy." Len smiles, too.

He turns back around and watches The Dealer effortlessly throw cards towards the players. Len scans his face, taking in every little detail, like the freckle under his eye that's bigger than the rest on his face. Who is he?

"Incoming," Theo whispers.

They all follow his gaze and spot Randall power-walking towards them.

"What've we done this time?" Al asks him.

"This isn't about you. I need to talk to Len," he says, keeping his eyes glued to his target.

Len looks back at him and then around the table,

"Alone!" Randall snaps.

"I won't be a minute," he says, looking everyone over again.

They walk a few paces away from the table before Randall begins, "I have an observation to share with you."

"Go on, and make it quick, they're suspicious."

"Before I tell you... What are you going to do for me in return?" Randall smirks.

Len rolls his eyes but appeases him. "What do you want?"

"I want to know where you four sneak off to in the kitchen." He glares.

"I can't tell you that," Len says, looking over at the table and seeing that they're all looking back at him.

"Then I can't tell you about the investigators that have just entered the staffroom," Randall replies and begins to walk off.

"Are they here for me?" Len catches his arm.

"Most definitely." He smirks and somehow squints his eyes even more.

Len mulls it over for a minute. "What are you going to do with the information I give you?"

"Keep it up here," he says, tapping his temple with a bony finger.

"Fine... We go up to the roof. Now tell me about the investigators."

"They have a file with your name on it."

"What else?" Len pushes.

"That's all I know." Randall smiles and walks away.

"Are you joking?" he shouts after him.

Randall ignores him, making his way to the staffroom to tell Atilla his newly discovered secret.

Len runs his hand through his ever-growing hair. *It'll soon be the same length as Jenk's was*, he thinks to himself. He walks back to the poker table and sits down.

"What was all that about?" Theo asks suspiciously.

"Nothing really, he's a dickhead," Len replies frankly.

They can tell he doesn't want to talk about it, and so the game continues.

Theo wins his first game ever, only because no-one could stand his sulking any more at never having won one. They let him win quite obviously, folding straight flushes and such, but he was too invested to notice.

Scott suggests going for a celebratory smoke and of course everyone agrees. Regret tugs at the sleeve of Len's overalls, like a needy child, as he remembers what he told Randall. He thinks about whether he should bring it up or not, and how he would even do it. He decides against telling them; he'll deal with it when the time comes.

Just like the first day they met, the nurses sit quietly in their chairs, staring interestingly at their new supply teachers, the powerful Detective Reinhold and the shrivelled Detective Shelley.

"Congratulations, you've completed your first week of

investigation school," Reinhold praises sarcastically. "Have you got anything useful to report back to us? Our body language expert said Len's too good at poker for him to even lie."

The nurses fall quiet and look nervously at each other; nobody knows anything about Len.

"Anything at all?" Reinhold pushes for an answer.

Atilla stands up to address him on behalf of all the nurses. "You see, Detective, Len is very difficult to control. We've already had a few incidents with him here at the hospital."

"Like what?" Detective Reinhold scowls and folds his arms over his chest.

Even Detective Shelley seems to have been awakened from his trance, as he looks hopelessly at Atilla.

"Well, he's been telling those stupid stories ever since he got here. Pirates, astronauts, mermaids. It's ridiculous. He ran through the hospital stark naked on Thursday-"

"Why?" Reinhold asks suspiciously.

"I'm not sure... Just to be distracting, I think," Atilla tries to answer.

"Distracting you from what?" Reinhold raises a quizzical eyebrow.

Atilla opens her mouth to answer, but suddenly realises that she doesn't have a clue, and she didn't even initially realise it was to distract them from something.

"Perhaps we could go in and have a word with him." Reinhold smirks condescendingly to Shelley, since the nurses are too stupid for this investigative work.

Shelley nods glumly.

"We're more than capable of handling him ourselves, Detective," Atilla states defiantly.

A quick knock on the door follows, and Randall pokes his head around the door. "Len is on the roof smoking weed," he tells them, looking at the detectives and then ducking out of the door again.

Detective Reinhold turns his head to look back at Atilla, looking smug at her just being proved wrong. "Shall we go and sort this out, Shelley?" he asks, keeping his eyes on Atilla.

Without having to reply, they both stand up from leaning on the desk, and exit the room, leaving the nurses in there to regroup their situation.

"Now... How do we get to the roof?" Reinhold asks himself aloud, looking up and down the corridor.

"There's a secret door in the kitchen," Randall snarls from his squatted position on the floor, next to the staffroom door.

Reinhold and Shelley both jump and spin around trying to find him, and then look down.

"How do you know that?" Reinhold demands, standing menacingly over Randall.

"Len told me." He flips to the page in his notebook that says it.

Reinhold snatches it out of his hand and they proceed to the kitchen.

"My notebook!" Randall wails as he stands up, his arm outstretched towards the detectives.

"Yeah, we saw them outside a coffee shop but we thought they were just people that looked like them. The whole band was in there, and we knew, but we didn't at the same time!" Len tells them about his trip to Amsterdam to see Tenacious Toes.

They all laugh. Al finishes off the spliff and throws it off the edge of the building.

"Did you ever meet them?" Theo asks.

"Yeah, we ended up back at their hotel. That's when Dizza

gave us the idea to try and find the answer through drugs. In hindsight, it wasn't our best decision to go along with."

Scott chuckles and throws his head back. "I would say it *was* your best decision. You see, Len, us two are lucky. We lived our lives to the max before getting chucked in here forever."

Len's smile drops from his face. "Yeah, lucky..."

The heavy door flings open and the two detectives square them all up. Shelley looks miserably at Al and she diverts her gaze to Len, who is now shaking uncontrollably and his eyes are darting everywhere.

"Hello, Len. We thought we'd pop in for a visit." Reinhold smiles deviously.

Len tries to get his words out. "H-h-h-how-w-w..."

Reinhold grabs Len by the arms and hauls him out of his seat, still stuttering, and drags him through the door. Shelley is left to round up the other three, which he does with no enthusiasm.

"Come on." He herds them with his long, thin arm.

They put up no fight, they were finished smoking anyway. Theo goes first, then Scott, then Al. Shelley's gaze sits on her for longer than needed.

"I'm going to need the key to this door," he says to her.

She looks at his face, taking in all the wrinkles and freckles as she fishes in her pockets for the key. She gently places it into his open, shaky palm.

"Thank you," he says, and holds her hands in his.

She slides them out of his grasp quickly and walks down the stairs and returns to the dayroom.

Reinhold takes Len to a private office, whilst Shelley locks the door to the roof and leaves the other three to go about their business.

"So, Len. The nurses here have just informed us about your fairy tales and naked shenanigans. What's going on?" Reinhold leans his elbows onto the desk to get into Len's personal space.

"How did you know we were up there?" He ignores the question.

"I can't divulge that information," Reinhold says sternly.

"It was Randall, wasn't it?"

"If that's the kid with the notepad, then yes."

Liam lets out a breath of disappointment and shakes his head. "Typical!" he says wearily.

Reinhold takes the notepad out in front of Len and begins to flick through it. "Wow, he's quite the organiser. It's no challenge to find all the dirt he has on you." Reinhold smirks at the pages and then at Len.

"Go on then," Len says confidently.

"Let's see here... *Len is alone in his room; he's fallen out with his friends.* Ooh, not good. What happened there?" Reinhold pretends to be interested.

"I just had my meeting with Atil... Mrs Hunning, and I wanted to be alone. We didn't fall out at all. Not quite the detective you thought he was, eh?" Len smiles at him.

Detective Shelley enters the room after struggling to lock the door. He stands behind Reinhold on the opposite side of the desk to Len, and says nothing.

"Okay then, let's see what else we have." Reinhold flicks through the pages.

He stops dead on a certain page, his eyes widening. He turns to Shelley and holds up the notebook for him to read. Shelley puts his glasses on the end of his nose and reads the scribbles frantically. The detectives look at each other in panic and then at Len.

"What is it?" Len asks.

"What do you know about your fellow patients, Len?" Reinhold asks cautiously.

"Not much... Why?" he asks again, confused.

Reinhold looks back to Shelley again and he nods slightly in reply. Reinhold turns back to Len and shakes his head.

"No reason. We'll need to talk to this... what's his name?"

"Randall."

"Yes, Randall. Could you tell him to come here, when you see him? We'll be waiting."

Len takes this as his cue to leave, which he does, and instantly spots Randall in the corridor. He angrily strides over to him,

"Len! Those detectives have my notebook!" Randall shouts to him as Len quickly gets closer and closer.

Len grabs Randall by the collar and drags him close to his face. "Why would you tell them we were up there?" he spits, through gritted teeth.

"I didn't know they were there!" he lies.

"Well, they've got your notebook, and they've read everything. They're waiting for you in that room." Len points to the door he's just emerged from. "It isn't looking good for you, *Randall*," Len snarls, shoving him backwards as he lets go of Randall's collar.

He gives him one last glare before he pushes past his shoulder and returns to the dayroom.

Randall gulps and slowly makes his way to the office door. He knocks gently a couple of times and pries open the door. When he steps in, both detectives are staring menacingly at him.

"H-hello," he stutters.

"Sit down," Reinhold orders.

Randall swiftly lands on the seat and tightly clamps his hands in between his knees.

Reinhold holds up the notebook and Randall tries to snatch it out of his hands, but Reinhold's reactions are too fast and Randall hopelessly claws at the air.

"What's your name?"

"Randall Savage, *SIR!*"

Reinhold flinches at the volume of his voice but quickly recovers. "Well, Randall. You won't be getting this notebook back, and I order you to stop snooping around other patients' business. We have an operation ongoing in here and we don't need you messing it up. Okay?" Reinhold explains.

"What operation?" Randall's eyes light up.

As if we'd tell a snitch, Reinhold thinks to himself; for obvious reason, he can't voice this opinion.

"We can't divulge that information. Once our operation is over, you're more than welcome to continue with your... endeavours. But until then, we *ask* you to stop playing detective for now." He emphasises 'ask', meaning 'order'.

Randall nods glumly at the floor.

"Last question. When Len came to get you, what was he like?" Reinhold leans onto the table.

"He was angry. He grabbed me by the collar and shouted in my face." Randall shivers at the memory of it.

"Okay." Reinhold nods.

"Can I go now?"

"Yes. We'll be dropping by again to check up on you, Mr Savage."

Randall's eyes pop with fear and he runs out of the room, slamming the door behind him.

Reinhold can't help but laugh a little at how much he'd managed to scare him, but Shelley doesn't see the funny side.

"That was a close one. Are you sure we can trust him not to say anything?" Shelley grumbles.

"I think so. He looks up to authority figures, he'll want to prove himself to us." Reinhold rubs his stubbled chin with the back of his fingers.

"And Len? We didn't even get to question him."

"We got under his skin, that's enough for now. Things might get heated with Randall after this, then we'll have our chance."

The detectives return to the staffroom, where some of the nurses are still discussing the meeting. Reinhold quickly addresses the room from the doorway.

"Your tactics aren't working if you have nothing useful for us yet. We'll be back next week, or whenever you give us a call to come in."

"What would you have us do instead?" Atilla asks, out of ideas.

"Whatever it takes," Reinhold replies, and the two of them leave the building promptly.

CHAPTER ELEVEN

There were many questions spiralling around Len's head in the shower this morning.

Do I really want to find out why I shouldn't be talking to Al?

What did they see in that notebook?

How am I going to get out of here?

Should I start telling the truth?

WHO IS THAT BEHIND ME?

He turns his head ever so slightly to the left, and pushes his side eye skills to capacity to see who it is hovering behind him. He still can't see, so he goes for the plunge and turns around. A big sigh of relief follows, once he sees DJ Gurns' gormless face in front of his.

Len carefully looks DJ over. "Are you okay?" he asks him.

DJ dribbles in reply.

Len looks around. There isn't anybody else in that row of showers, but he can hear singing and whistling from behind the dividing wall.

He tries again. "DJ?"

Out of nowhere, DJ snaps out of his trance and charges at Len with arms outstretched, and screaming unintelligible words. Thanks to his quick reflexes, Len slides across the wet floor out of the way of DJ's death grip just in the nick of time. Unfortunately, because of these reflexes, DJ skids straight into the wall, hitting his head on the shower tap. He falls to the floor unconscious and bleeding badly from his head.

The other patients peer around the wall to see what all the commotion is. Once Randall sees the scene, he runs straight to the door to inform Adesso that Len has injured DJ in the showers.

"What happened, Len?" Scott appears from around the corner, the water dripping down from his mullet onto his flat chest.

"He ran at me! I moved out the way and he hit his head on the tap!" Len frantically tries to explain.

Adesso pushes his way through the quickly forming crowd. He looks down at the body, then back up at Len.

"You're coming with me." Adesso drags Len out of the shower room and informs the other nurses.

DJ is taken out on a stretcher and wheeled to the on-site hospital building for further treatment. Meanwhile, Len is strapped into a strait jacket in the hallway of the men's dorm, with nothing else for cover.

By now, the rumours have already spread throughout the hospital and people have started lining the hall to get a glimpse of the man who killed DJ in the showers. Len desperately tries to explain away his guilt to anyone who'll listen.

Big Al comes barging through the stairwell doors, being led through the corridor by Theo and Scott,

"Get out my way!" she demands, as she pushes patients into the wall to get past.

"What are you looking at, eh? Piss off!" The three of them

begin to disperse the ogling crowd. "Go on, off you pop! Don't let me catch you in this hall again!" Big Al shouts in Randall's face as he jots down in his new notepad.

She rushes over to Len and begins untying the jacket behind him.

"Al, what are you doing? I'm gonna be in even more trouble if you do this!" Len squirms.

"No, you won't, they can't do this to you," she states, continuing to untie him. "Theo, will you get him some overalls, please?"

He scuttles off into his room, returning with a fresh jumpsuit, neatly folded.

Once freed, Len quickly pulls on his overalls, trying to keep as much modesty as he possibly can, which, by this point, is not a lot.

Adesso thunders down the strip from the opposite end of the corridor. "What do you think you're doing? He's been restrained for a reason!" he barks.

"You couldn't just leave him there like that, he had no clothes on!"

"He's dangerous! He needed to be restrained right away," Adesso argues.

"Have you actually asked him what happened?" she shouts, standing on her tiptoes to get in his face.

Adesso pauses, thinking, *oh yeah, I probably should've*, but the anger burns up inside him again, releasing all the steam and common sense along with it.

"I don't need to ask. It's obvious he bludgeoned DJ to death." He scowls.

"With what?" Al shrugs, waiting for him to come up with something.

"I don't need to answer to any of you!" he roars, pushing Al against the wall with one swoop of his arm.

The patients freeze in dismay, looking from Al to Adesso. But the big nurse is on a roll now. He grabs Len tightly by the shoulder and drags him out of the corridor.

"Where are you taking him?" Scott shouts to them before they disappear.

"The basement!" Adesso shouts back in reply, without turning around.

Al rubs her arm and stands up. "We have to get him out of there ASAP," she says worriedly.

"None of us have ever been to the basement before, so how would we even pull it off?" Theo asks.

"We need to look at those blueprints again," she says, and the three of them rush back to the secret dining room.

Slotted into the underside of the table are the master blueprints. Al spreads the map across the table and the three of them stand around, trying to find the basement.

"I don't see it anywhere..." Theo mumbles, while biting his fingernails.

"Yeah, it doesn't look like it's on here," Scott adds.

"Fuck." Al runs her hands through her hair. "I don't even know if there would be a separate set of blueprints for the basement."

"What are we gonna do?" Theo slumps down into a chair in defeat.

"I'm going to go and speak to Atilla... try and sort this mess out," Al says, thumping her fist onto the table defiantly.

"What?" Theo sits up abruptly. "That'll never work! She's a witch!"

"There's a few other things she is as well, but she's not completely unreasonable."

"We'll wait for you in the dayroom," Scott says, following behind her out of the door.

Al knocks on the door to Atilla's office.

Her hefty voice bellows, and rattles the frosted window in the door: *"ENTAAAAH!"*

Al smiles from around the door and Atilla flashes her a quick half smile back before her face goes back to normal.

"What is it, Ace?" Atilla asks, not looking up from her paperwork anymore.

"Have you heard about what happened with Len?"

"Yes. Terrible business."

"He didn't hurt him, you know. He hit his head when he slipped."

"That's not what it looked like. And besides, we can't go on hearsay, you weren't even there."

"I know, but I know Len and he wouldn't do something like that."

Atilla finally looks up from her paperwork and raises a suspicious eyebrow at Al.

"You've only known him for a week. How could you possibly know him as well as you say?"

"He's not a bad person."

"Again, you don't know that. He needs to be punished, Ace, and that's what's going to happen."

Al continues to sit and think instead of leaving, as she hasn't heard everything she needs to.

"How's DJ, then?" she asks Atilla.

"Fine."

"Everyone's saying he's dead."

"Well, he's not," she says, concentrating more on ticking boxes on her paperwork than on Al.

"What happened to him? Apparently, he just went mental." She describes what Scott told her.

This startles Atilla and she looks up again. "Who's said that?" She tries not to sound worried.

"Everyone who saw it," Al lies, knowing she's onto something.

"Well... we've been trialling a new medicine for him... Perhaps it didn't work as we'd expected. We'll have to look further into the matter." She goes back to her paperwork.

Al doesn't even know what to say. She knows they set it up somehow, but she doesn't want Atilla to know that just yet.

"Alright, erm... can you at least let me know when Len will be coming back?" She stands up from her chair.

"When we're done with him." Atilla smiles so widely that Al can see her black wisdom teeth.

Al nods in reply and leaves the room. She stands in the corridor for a moment to gather her thoughts and then meets the boys in the dayroom.

"Well?" Scott asks hopefully.

"I couldn't get him out. I don't know when he'll be back, either."

Scott and Theo crumple into themselves with disappointment. They were more than ready for another exciting mission.

"We just have to hope he's okay down there," Theo mumbles.

The three of them lie defeatedly on the couches around the TV, the absence of DJ twisting the knobs making them feel even worse.

Eucalyptus comes over to join them, her usual happy self. "Who died?" she jokes.

"Maybe DJ, and maybe Len, too," Theo sulks.

"Actually, Atilla said DJ is fine. But Len... I don't know," Al corrects.

"What's happened?" Eucalyptus says, shocked, sounding more serious now.

They explain this morning's events to her and she watches with wide eyes and often mouths their words along with them, as she tries to concentrate.

"... So now we don't know what to do. We don't have blueprints to the basement and we don't know anyone that's been there before, so there's no way we can form a plan," Al finishes.

Eucalyptus purses her lips for a moment, then quietly says, "I know someone."

"You do? Who is it?" Scott sits up from his slump.

"You wouldn't have met her. She's not allowed down here," Eucalyptus begins.

"Have I met her? Is she in the women's common room?" Al asks simultaneously, trying urgently to find a solution.

"She's not allowed in there, either." Eucalyptus smirks.

"Who is she, then?"

"She's known as... GBH."

CHAPTER TWELVE

E ucalyptus and Al make their way to the women's floor, leaving Scott and Theo in the dayroom.

"If she can't go anywhere, where do they keep her?" Al asks as they stroll down the corridor.

"There are a few things this place tries to hide. The basement is one of them, and the extremely violent patients are the other. This place already gets a bad rep, they don't need an inspector getting murdered in here, too," Eucalyptus explains. "So, they keep her in a secret sound-proofed room at the end of this corridor."

"How do you know about this?" Al asks her.

Eucalyptus stops abruptly and turns to Al. "If I told you that, I'd have to kill you." She smiles.

Al smiles back. "I don't doubt that you would."

They continue walking until they reach the barred window at the end. Al looks around and doesn't see anything that could be a secret room, but she notes that there is a wide length of wall that has no use.

"I'm guessing it's behind here." Al points to the wall.

"You're dead right," Eucalyptus confirms.

"How do we get in then?"

Eucalyptus bends down and flicks the switch on the empty plug socket. The wall pings forward slightly, allowing them to pull it open to reveal a big metal door.

"Whoa... Was not expecting something like that in a place like this." Al ogles.

"I know. They're a lot more sinister than you think."

"WHO'S THERE? LET ME OUT!" They hear it only slightly through the thick door, but they can tell it was a very aggressive shout.

Eucalyptus slides the tiny metal window open and they both squeeze up to the door to look into the room. Inside, they see a giant blob wrapped up tightly in a strait jacket. The room is completely padded with soft material and there is no bed in sight, just a toilet.

"Jesus," Al mumbles to herself.

"WHAT ARE YOU LOOKING AT? COME IN HERE AND LET ME OUT!" GBH screams at them. She tries to stand up, but the lack of available arm movement just makes her roll around the floor like a broken weeble. Al tries to stifle her laughter at the sight.

She puts her mouth through the window. "It's Eucalyptus! This is Al, she needs your help."

"AND HOW AM I SUPPOSED TO HELP WHEN I'M TIED UP IN HEEEEEERE?" she screams and goes mental, throwing herself around the room.

Al steps back from the door and doubles over in quiet laughter. Tears drip from her eyes onto the floor. Eucalyptus turns to her and has a little giggle herself before shoving her mouth back through the window.

"Please stop shouting, the nurses don't know we're here.

She needs to know about the basement," Eucalyptus explains to her.

"The basement," GBH repeats, the first thing she hasn't shouted.

"Yeah, her mate Len's just been sent down there."

"Well, he isn't comin' back!" she strops. "He'll probably end up like me."

I doubt that, Al thinks to herself. She goes back over to the door to get the information herself.

"I just need to know what it looks like, what the security's like down there, where we can expect to find him. We're going to try and break him out." Al pushes for answers.

"*AND WHY WOULD I HELP YOU?*" GBH screams back in reply.

"Why not? You've got nothing else to do," Al says, matter-of-factly.

GBH goes silent, trying to think of an insult, but she can't; Al's right.

"Fine... There's a guard stationed in a security box at the bottom of the stairs. There's a big sliding cell door that he has to open. Then there's a lot of twisting alleyways full of giant pipes and cables. Once you get past them, you won't be able to miss him." She calmly maps it out.

"Thanks," Al says, ready to leave.

"He'll be hung up by his neck probably," GBH mutters, but loud enough for them to hear.

Al looks at Eucalyptus and she looks back worriedly.

"Thanks, G," she says, without looking back inside the room, and slides the window closed again. She pushes the wall back into place and the switch on the plug socket flips back automatically.

"We need to move quickly then," Al says sternly.

Eucalyptus frowns. "How are we supposed to get past the cell door?"

"I haven't even thought about it, I just want to get him out," Al says, as she begins making her way to the dayroom to inform the lads.

She explains everything to them, and they're just as eager to barge in there without a plan. They stomp down the corridor towards the basement stairs, all with a determined look on their face. Eucalyptus jogs next to them, trying to keep up and talk some sense into them.

"You don't even have a plan! What are you going to do? You'll end up in there with him! Please just think about it for a minute!" she pleads to them all.

Al stops and so does the whole group behind her. She turns to Eucalyptus and says to her quietly, "There's no time to stop and think about it. He's already been in there for a few hours. You heard what GBH said. We might already be too late."

Just then, Paul appears from the basement stairs and saunters down the corridor.

"Hey guys! What you doing in the corridor?" he chirps.

"Erm, just talking. We're wondering how Len's doing," Scott cuts in, before anyone else can.

"He's... okay..." Paul tries to smile.

"What were you doing down there?" Eucalyptus moves playfully closer to him.

"I'm on the brew run. Ten sugars, no milk, is what the security guard asked for! How weird is that?" Paul laughs with them all.

"Well, if you've got loads to do, I can take it to him for you." Al smiles innocently.

"Patients aren't allowed down there, I'm afraid." He shakes his head.

"Oh, come on, Paul! I thought you liked Len?" Theo says.

"I do! But... he hurt DJ." He looks ashamed for both him and Len.

"Do you *really* believe that?" Eucalyptus gets even closer to him.

"No." He smiles and blushes.

"Then let's help him!" She celebrates.

"Come on, Pauuuuuul!" everyone sings, watching him become more bashful.

"Paul-*ie*, Paul-*ie*, Paul-*ie*!" They begin to chant around him, pumping their fists in the air.

He gives in and laughs. "Okay, okay! Let's help him."

They all cheer and he goes to make the odd mixture of tea and ten sugars. He reappears in the corridor holding a mug and joins the group again.

"Let's try it," Eucalyptus orders.

He reluctantly hands her the mug and she takes a big sip. She pulls a face like she just sucked on a lemon and spits it back into the mug. "That's disgusting!"

"I can't give him that now!" Paul exclaims.

"Why not? She's probably made it taste better," Scott laughs.

Eucalyptus winks at him and they turn their attention back to Paul.

"So, what are you gonna say?" Al asks.

"That Mrs Hunning wants him for a meeting," Paul says, quite happy with himself.

"Good one! Go get 'em, girl!" Scott hollers and smacks him on the bum as he makes his way to the stairs, the tea nearly spilling out the sides of the mug with the force of it.

There's no way he would have gotten away with that had it been any other nurse – that's why everybody likes Paul.

They wait nervously in the corridor for fifteen minutes, not sure who they could expect to come back up the stairs. They hear footsteps from behind the door and they all grab hold of each other in anticipation. Paul's head pops out first, looking around the corridor to check no nurses are there. He emerges fully from the door and a haggard-looking Len follows. His overalls are slashed and he has a shiny purple bruise around his eye.

"Len!" they all shout and surround him with a big group hug that even Paul joins in with.

"Thank you, Paul, you're a literal lifesaver!" Eucalyptus gives him a big 'thank you' squeeze.

The others pat him on the arm or the face and he rejects the praise even though he loves it.

"I'd do it again for any one of you," he smiles, "but I have to go, I can't get caught with you all. Please don't tell anyone it was me."

"We won't, but what about that security guard?" Al remembers.

Paul looks horrified. "Oh no!" He covers his mouth with his hand. "It's a good job I only put eight spoonfuls of sugar and two spoonfuls of sleeping pills in his tea then." He grins.

They all cheer for him again and he receives another round of pats on the back before he leaves to continue his tea run for the staff.

Al turns to Len. "Right, well, we can't hide you forever but we should do for as long as we can. I think it'll be worse if they go down and see you aren't there."

"Yeah, they need to know you're out before they see you up here," Scott agrees.

They take Len back up to the room he shares with Mehzah and gently lay him down on the bed.

"What happened down there?" Al asks sympathetically.

"Adesso tortured me and then he tied my hands together

over a pipe and left me there," he explains, tears welling up in his eyes.

Al sits on the bed next to him and holds his hand gently. "Is there anything we can do for you?" she asks him.

"You've done more than enough getting me out of there. Thank you so much."

"No problem, mate, you did nothing wrong," Scott tells him. Al and Theo nod in agreement.

"We're going downstairs to clear your name. Do you want someone to stay here with you, or do you want to be alone?" Al asks.

"I'd like to be alone," he says quietly.

They all give him a quick hug and stride triumphantly to the dayroom. Their plan is to gather all the patients who know Len and urge them to persuade the nurses he did nothing wrong. Whether that'll work, they have no idea.

CHAPTER THIRTEEN

I t takes the gang half an hour to set up their protest. They recruit their patients and set up the dayroom in the same way the nurses do for meetings. Mr Lewis, now fully recovered from his trance, sits patiently in the semicircle, waiting for his moment to repay the favour to Len. Eucalyptus sits next to him, cross-legged on her chair, shouting directions at the other patients: "Big scowls, everybody! Look angry!"

Once everything is in place, Al begins Phase 2, Bring in the Beasts! She throws the patients a thumbs-up and they reply with their own; everybody's ready. She knocks on the staffroom door and opens the door without hesitation.

"We have a meeting set up in the dayroom that we'd like you to attend," she says, stern-faced.

The nurses look at each other with disbelief. Atilla lets out a big, condescending laugh. "I can't wait to see this!" she scoffs and pushes past Al in the doorway.

"Oh, by the way..." She turns to Atilla, who also turns around to hear what Al has to say. "The Inspector should be here any minute." She smiles.

The gang had told Paul of their idea and he loved it, and thought, why not go a step further? Invite the Inspector! If there's one thing Paul hates it's mistreatment, and the only person that can help this place is an outsider.

Atilla's face drops and she tries to call off the meeting, but just on cue, a guard strolls down the corridor, Inspector in tow. He's a very thin, tall man, at least seven foot. He has small rectangular glasses and big blue eyes that are as soft as butter. He knows vaguely of the investigation going on in the hospital, but he only knows what the nurses want him to hear.

"Inspectoooor..." Atilla tries not to sound flushed. "How wonderful to see you." She walks over and shakes his hand.

"Thank you. I must say I was quite surprised by this unofficial meeting, but nonetheless, I'm intrigued to see what it's all about." He smiles.

"Everything is set up in the dayroom, sir. We'll be in shortly." She plasters a fake smile across her own face.

The Inspector pushes his glasses up his nose and strides towards the dayroom.

"Call the detectives." Atilla's face drops into a menacing scowl. "You've caused enough trouble in here as is." She squares up to Al before stomping toward the dayroom.

Only the Inspector is provided with a chair, forcing the other nurses to stand behind him whilst a semicircle of dishevelled patients surround him on their own thrones. Al stands up to commence the meeting and address the room,

"Hello everyone, thank you for coming to the first patient-run meeting," she begins.

The Inspector looks startled. Unaware of who had actually organised the meeting, he turns quickly to the nurses behind him, and then places his full attention on Al.

"We're here today to clear the name of patient Len

Moscow, who was falsely imprisoned and tortured for a crime he did not commit."

The patients in the circle chant and wave their fists in the air at the nurses, especially Atilla and Adesso.

The Inspector pushes his glasses onto his nose again and opens his notebook. "Torture? Are you insane?" Atilla recoils at her poor choice of words.

"I would like to hear what they have to say, Mrs Hunning," the Inspector states, without looking back at her.

"In the men's showers this morning, another patient, known as DJ, had a psychotic episode, that I have the right to believe was caused by drugs supplied by the hospital."

"*RIDICULOUS!*" Atilla screams and everyone can sense the sheer anger in her voice.

"Shhh." The Inspector quietens her down calmly.

"He attempted to attack Len Moscow but he managed to get out of the way just in time. Unfortunately, because of this, DJ slipped on the wet tiles and hit his head against the shower tap. The small amount of blood on the tap reinforces this scenario," Al concludes.

"Or he grabbed him by the head and smashed it into the tap!" Adesso shouts.

"Shush!" The Inspector turns around now.

Adesso pushes his tongue into his cheek and crosses his arms, trying to stay quiet.

"We thought you'd say something like that. That's why we've collected a group of patients who know Len, and know he isn't they type of person who would want to harm anybody." She gestures to the beginning of the semicircle.

First up is Randall. He wrings his hands as he stands up nervously, his knees shaking and hardly supporting his weight. He looks over at Atilla, who looks very displeased. He gulps down his fear and looks at the Inspector.

"I've known Len since he arrived. Despite some patients telling him to 'stay away' from me, he didn't. He talked to me and we trusted each other with our secrets," he mumbles quietly.

Al raises an eyebrow to Scott who's sitting a few seats down from her and he reciprocates the surprise.

"He wouldn't hurt a fly..." His eyes start darting now as he remembers Len grabbing him by the collar. He sits down again.

Eucalyptus stands up next. "I love Len! He's such a free spirit, and so down to earth and one with nature. I've never seen him hurt anyone or even raise his voice at another person," she explains. "And you've got to admit, he's extremely sexy!" she adds on the end for good luck. She smiles and sits down.

Next up is Mr Lewis, their ace card. He slowly wobbles himself upright, with a little help from Eucalyptus, and salutes the Inspector, who bashfully mimics him.

"Good day to you, sir. I hope by now you understand what a fantastic young man our Len is. He brightened up this hospital with his wonderful stories and, most heroic of all, he saved my life when I, too, was sent to the basement to be tortured."

"Oh dear. Can you tell me what happened to you, sir?" the Inspector asks him politely.

Mr Lewis teeters a little bit and digs out a white handkerchief from his pocket to wipe the tears from his eyes. "It was horrible. I wouldn't wish it on my worst enemy." He begins to cry. "It was worse than when I was a prisoner of war in the Forties."

He can't regain his composure after this statement and he is helped back into his chair, with Eucalyptus moving to comfort him.

Mr Lewis was never a 'traditional' prisoner of war. He refers to his innocent mind that is forever trapped in a distorted, unfamiliar body. His childhood memories are replaced by graphic scenes of a brutal war.

Al takes control of the meeting again after the rest of the semicircle has voiced their positive opinions on Len and a couple of extra stories about the basement.

"But of course, there's only one person's account that really matters – Len's," Al says conclusively.

Theo finally enters the room with Len trailing behind him with a blanket draped over his shoulders. He looks worse than he did when they rescued him.

"*WHAT'S HE DOING UP HERE?*" Atilla demands to know.

"*YOU'RE DEAD, BOY!*" Adesso charges over to him.

The Inspector intercepts just in the nick of time. "Calm down please," he says, placing a steady hand on Adesso's hard, muscular chest. He can feel Adesso's forceful, heavy breathing pushing back against his pale, feeble hand. It's a good job Adesso respects authority, otherwise the Inspector would no longer be alive.

Len slowly reaches a chair and sits down, looking around at everyone, not sure what's going on.

"Len, some patients have told their stories about being in the basement. Do you want to tell the Inspector yours?" Al asks him softly.

He glances over at the kind-looking Inspector and nods his head solemnly.

"I was dragged down there, taken through a maze of pipes and cables. Then he tried to drown me in a dirty sink full of water. He beat me and tied my hands above a pipe on the ceiling and continued to punch me in the stomach. He said he was going to kill me," Len explains.

"There's still time yet," Adesso snaps angrily.

The Inspector writes this down and turns to the nurses disapprovingly.

"Surely you don't believe this, Inspector? We've told you about his outlandish stories before, he's in Len World." Atilla tuts and shakes her head.

"I would like to see this basement, please, Mrs Hunning," the Inspector asks.

"There is no basement." Atilla shrugs. "I think you're forgetting that you're in a hospital full of mentally insane patients, Inspector."

"It's through the door that says NO ENTRY, you can't miss it," Al directs.

The Inspector exits the room without another word and tries to open the door in question. It doesn't budge.

"Do you have the key, Mrs Hunning?" he asks.

She hands it over to him after searching for it in the staffroom.

"Is this the only key?"

"Yes," she replies.

Instead of opening the door with it, he returns to the dayroom and addresses the patients. He holds the key up to them,

"I don't need to see this basement that you speak of, I can see how much it terrifies you all. I will be taking control of this key, the only key, so you don't have to worry about being sent down there again."

The patients cheer and hug each other as the nurses stand in the doorway, trying to get the Inspector out of the building.

"We respect your decision, Inspector, but what do you propose we do with Mr Moscow?" Atilla asks, as she ushers him down the corridor towards the main entrance.

"Leave him be. I don't think he did any harm to that boy."

Just as the Inspector closes himself into his car and reverses out of his parking space, the undercover police car enters the car park and Detective Shelley and Detective Reinhold appear from the gleaming BMW.

"Thank God you're here, it's all going to pot," Atilla pleads to them.

She explains the situation to them in the staffroom, and they, too, agree that Len should be left alone for now. They still have one trick up their sleeve.

In the dayroom, Al gives Len a big, victorious bear hug. He flinches with the pain but doesn't mind one bit.

"I'm so proud of you, Len." She smiles and places her hand around his cheek.

"Thanks. I'm really proud of you, too, for everything you've done for me, and now the entire hospital," he gushes, with tears in his eyes.

"You really need to get out of here, Len. Do whatever it takes," she orders him.

Len stares directly into her eyes and he understands what she means completely. He nods and Al does, too.

Mr Lewis comes over to them and shakes Len's limp hand. They talk about their mistreatment in the basement and comfort each other that it's over now.

"Ace!" Atilla shouts from the dayroom doorway.

They look over to see her standing there with her arms folded, the tower of a man that is Detective Reinhold looming behind her.

"The detectives would like a word with you." She smirks.

All eyes are on Al again. "Don't worry," she says to them, and makes her way to the staffroom with Atilla and Reinhold.

The atmosphere in there is completely different to the

uplifted spirits of the dayroom. The detectives and nurses alike all look very unhappy and disappointed.

"What do you think you're doing?" Detective Reinhold asks her.

"What do you mean?" She pretends not to know, shifting from one foot to the other.

"Breaking patients out, sticking up for them. This is not what you're here for."

"Why not? The patients are treated horrendously here. If I can make a difference, then that's what I'm going to do," Al explains passionately.

Detective Shelley finally speaks. "My girl, you've always been strong-willed, but your job was to catch Len out."

"I can't catch him out because he didn't do it! He would have told me by now."

"We don't know that for sure... But our next move will definitely get the truth out of him." Reinhold smirks at her.

"What is it? For God's sake!" She rolls her eyes.

"Operation Ace in the Hole." He smiles more deviously this time.

"No. I'm not doing it." She shakes her head disgustedly.

"Yes, you are," Detective Shelley orders her.

"You can't make me!" She crosses her arms.

The detectives look at each other and then at Adesso. He nods in compliance.

CHAPTER FOURTEEN

Atilla appears in the doorway of the dayroom. She loudly unbolts one of the doors from the wall, making sure all eyes are on her. She snaps it shut and goes to do the same to the other door. Behind her, the sight of Adesso dragging Al out of the staffroom with tape over her mouth is enough to send all of the patients flying towards the doors, insisting that they let her go.

"Where is he taking her?" Scott demands to know.

Atilla snaps the last door in place and smiles. "You didn't think we'd *really* have just *one* key to the basement, did you?" she says, with a sneering laugh.

A complete riot begins in the dayroom and Atilla struggles to control even one of the patients. Chairs get thrown at the door, that were originally aimed at Atilla. The poker table gets flipped and the TV is pushed off the wooden table and smashes into millions of shards across the floor.

"*THAT'S ENOUGH!*" she screams, so loudly that everybody covers their ears and comes to a halt. "There's only one way you can save her this time."

"What is it? Anything!" Theo pleads.

She points an accusing finger at Len and says, scowling, "You need to tell the truth about the night of the murder, and if you don't, she won't be coming out of there alive! We've just about had it with you. The sooner you're out of here and in jail, the better."

The patients look hopefully at Len, all pleading inside their head that just this once he will manage to tell the truth. He looks around and, although he knows he has no choice but to say he'll do it, he contemplates his options.

"Okay. I'll do it." He hangs his head in defeat. "But... I want to see her out and know that she'll be safe before I say a single word to you," he demands.

"Fine." Atilla smirks, the plan had worked perfectly. "We'll set up your meeting with Detective Reinhold in, say... five minutes." She looks at her watch and then back up at Len.

He nods glumly and she unlocks the doors without letting any of the patients leave the room. She returns with a team of orderlies equipped with dust pans and brushes to clean up the mess, as well as Adesso, who is still holding onto Al's wrists behind her back. Len only has time to give her a quick hug before Reinhold beckons him into the office from down the corridor.

"Please tell them everything, Len," Al says to him.

"I will." He holds her face in his hands for a second before heading towards the office by himself.

"Welcome back, Len," Reinhold begins, sitting behind the same tattered oak desk.

"I'm ready to tell you everything, the full truth," he says, taking in a deep breath of stuffy air.

"Okay, great," Reinhold says, readying his pen and paper. "Start from when you heard the screaming," he guides.

"Well, by this point, we were all really high on shrooms and we'd smoked some weed, too. Flic had just been for a 'wild wee' as we call it, in the forest. She came back and said something about hallucinating this giant white rabbit and she wanted to follow it, so we did," Len begins to explain,

"We were walking down the trail through the forest and that's when we heard screaming. For some reason we decide to follow it and see what was going on. I can't say what the others saw but I witnessed myself doing the act, to that boy that was reported missing, Ryan. I never spoke about that night with any of the others, apart from Flic."

"That's all well and good, Len. But how do I know you haven't just gotten this from the book?" Reinhold asks, once he's finished writing his notes.

"I've never read it. I was arrested just before it was released. But I know something that wasn't in the book..."

"Go on." Reinhold waits patiently.

"I know how Gaz was really killed..." He begins to tear up and shakes his head at the floor.

The anticipative silence is too much for Len to handle and he can't help but break down in floods of tears. Reinhold passes him a handkerchief across the desk, which he takes gratefully and covers his eyes with it for a moment, letting the material soak up the river of regretful tears.

"This is why I can't talk about it." He laughs sadly.

"Take your time," Reinhold says, becoming softer with Len at last.

Len clears his throat and wipes his eyes again. "A few days before Flic died... I spoke to her about the night of the murder..." He begins to cry silently this time. "And she told me that... that she remembered that it was actually her. I don't know what she said she did in the book, but this is what she confessed to me on her deathbed.

"After Gaz had left, she was so paranoid about him coming back and harming us that she just had to go and find him to make sure he wasn't lurking in the bushes close by. I don't think she even knew what she was going to do if she did find him. But, as we all know, she did, and just out of pure fear she... she hit him with a stone she'd picked up on the way."

"She did mention a stone, but we didn't find anything at the crime scene," Reinhold interrupts.

"I know, you wouldn't have. She tossed it into the lake down the road to cover her tracks. But the whole white rabbit thing was just a lie she created to get us all to the crime scene, to make it look like she had just discovered it herself. I told her to stage it as self-defence when she said she wanted to write about it. I promised I would never tell anybody." He sighs and holds his head in his hands.

Reinhold compares the story against the evidence they had and it checks out.

"Please forgive me, Flic," Len cries to himself.

Reinhold hears this and now he understands; it was love that was holding Len back from telling the truth. He walks around the desk and puts his arms around Len's shoulders. Len embraces him tightly and cries heavily, covering Reinhold's blazer in tears and saliva.

"I never wanted to have to do this," Len sobs.

"I know it's hard, Len. But you did the right thing," Reinhold comforts him. "We really appreciate your effort. We can arrange your release date for as soon as possible."

"Can I go back to my mum and dad?" Len's eyes light up with hope and tears.

"Of course." Reinhold nods, seeing Len as just an innocent

teenager, much like his own son, for the first time since the investigation started.

"Thank you, Detective. I know I should have told the truth much sooner, but I couldn't bring myself to break my last promise to her." He begins to cry again.

Not wanting to inflict any more emotional pain on the poor boy, Reinhold brings Shelley up to speed and together, they guide Len back into the corridor where Atilla stands smugly waiting, with the patients all crammed into the doorway, ordered not to leave the dayroom.

Seeing Len in tears makes her think that he's on his way to jail, so she slowly claps.

"It's finally happened, he's admitted it!" she sings.

"You're right, Mrs Hunning. He told the truth. We would like you to schedule his release for seven a.m. tomorrow morning, when he'll be sent back to his parent's house," Reinhold orders.

Atilla's mouth drops open in astonishment. "What?" She just about manages to push the word out of her fat mouth.

The patients cheer. Scott picks up Al and throws her into the air. They're all crying happy tears for Len. He notices them and he can't help but smile, which looks out of place on his blotchy red face that's still wet through with tears. He runs over to them and they pick him up and carry him over their heads and parade him around the dayroom singing, *For He's a Jolly Good Fellow*, as a fuck-you to Atilla. Even the detectives can't help but laugh.

"I knew he couldn't have done it. My daughter is never wrong about people," Shelley says to Reinhold, in a hushed voice.

"You know, Shelley, you're looking healthier already." Reinhold compliments him on his newly acquired touch of colour to his skin.

"I have nothing to worry about anymore, I can relax. The case is over and my daughter will be home safe by tomorrow morning." He smiles contentedly.

That night is full of celebrations. The hospital has never in its history held so much joy inside of it. Since the nurses are all too busy working through Len's release forms to keep an eye on the patients, Al manages to sneak the gang back up to the roof, along with Eucalyptus and Mr Lewis, using the key that Detective Shelley gave back to her.

"To Len!" Mr Lewis prompts the toast.

"To Len!" they repeat, and clink their plastic cups together.

They take a sip and most of them flinch at the way it burns their throat on the way down.

"Ugh! What the hell is this?" Theo spits it out.

"I'm not too sure, I found it in Atilla's stash," Scott says.

"Atilla's moustache?" Theo jokes.

"I'm not gonna miss jokes like that," Len teases, but Theo takes it slightly to heart.

"We're gonna miss you!" Eucalyptus smiles at Len.

"I'll miss you guys, too. I'm worried how you're going to cope without me, though," he replies, looking at the group.

"We've got no TV anymore, but we still have our daily poker game!" Scott laughs.

Len remembers the poker games he played in his short stay here.

"You know what I've just realised? I've never seen 'The Dealer' anywhere other than the poker table," he quizzes.

Al shuffles awkwardly on her seat, hoping someone else will take the podium on this one.

"I hadn't noticed," Scott ponders.

"You don't notice much, though, to be fair," Al laughs.

"True," Scott agrees with a chuckle.

By eleven o'clock, Mr Lewis, Eucalyptus and Theo have all gone to bed, wanting to be fresh for the morning to see Len off. Leaving just a drunken Al, Scott and Len on the roof, still drinking, laughing and chatting.

"Who fancies a spliff to get us to sleep?" Scott puts the feelers out.

"Defo," Len replies quickly. "Got to go out on a big one, haven't I?"

They smoke, making them even more twisted than they already were.

"I really want to say thank you to you guys. You've made this whole thing bearable," Len gushes.

"We've enjoyed being with you, too, Len. You made things much more exciting in here," Scott slurs.

Al nods. "We're also glad you're leaving, though. You deserve to be able to live the rest of your life in peace now, you've been through a lot."

"Yeah..." Len nods too.

"I'm gonna have to go to bed now, guys. It's been a pleasure." Scott stands up from his chair, extending his arms to embrace Len in a hug.

Len stands up and gives Scott the hug he asked for and they embrace for a long time, patting each other on the back and slurring words into each other's ears.

"Are you coming or staying up here?" Scott asks, just before he disappears through the door.

Len looks at Al for her answer.

"We'll come down in a minute. I want to have my chance to say goodbye to Len." She winks at him.

"Sweet. See you in the morning." He smiles dumbly before leaving the pair alone.

Len sits down next to Al and they smile at each other silently for a moment.

"Are you excited about tomorrow, then?" she asks finally.

"Of course I am," he says, his smile dropping quicker than expected.

"What's wrong?" she asks.

It takes him a while to pluck up the courage to say what he's been thinking about all night. "I just hate that I had to lie like that." He drops his head in shame.

"In your meeting? What did you say?" she wonders.

"You promise you won't say anything?" Len worries.

"I promise." She smiles. "I don't care that you lied, Len. I'm no saint, either. I told you to do whatever it took."

He nods and again has to build up the courage to say it.

"I blamed it all on Flic. Told them I made her write that it was self-defence."

"Was it not?"

"It wasn't Flic at all." He can't bring himself to look at her.

"Who was it then?" She panics, but tries to look calm.

"Me..." he says quietly.

Al's hands begin to shake and she can't control her breathing. "I don't understand, Len," she says brokenly.

"I knew that it was me as soon as it happened. No one believed me at first, thinking I was just being weirdly self-centred. Flic was so worried about me when she knew she didn't have long left. She said she'd write a book about it, and take the blame for me, since it wouldn't make a difference to her anymore," Len explains glumly.

"She really did that for you?" Al asks, her voice now a mere whisper.

"We loved each other so much," he says, as his eyes begin to well with tears again.

There's silence for what feels like forever as Al tries to think of how to ask him.

"Len... If you killed him, why did you do it?"

"I was just scared. I wasn't in a good frame of mind at the time. It's the biggest regret of my life... Apart from letting Flic take the rap for me." He shakes his head, sending the tears spinning off his face onto the floor.

Al can see how much he's hurting by it, and somehow, in this short amount of time, she, too, has developed romantic feelings for Len and doesn't want to see him in pain.

"I don't think any differently of you, Len. You did what you needed to do." She smiles slightly.

He picks up his head and looks deeply into her eyes. They're so close to each other now, and they can both feel the magnetic pull that's forcing their heads to gravitate closer and closer until their lips brush past each other's gently. Len pulls away first and smiles to himself.

"What are you smiling at?" she asks, a smile on her own face now as well.

"I was just thinking... If you were getting out of here as well, I'd love to take you on a date." He rubs the back of his neck shyly.

I wish he knew, Al thinks to herself.

"So, go on. Tell me an outrageous story about you, if you're not the saint that you look like," Len teases her, poking a finger into her side.

"All right!" She laughs, recoiling from his devil finger. "I come from a very straight-laced family... If they keep pushing you to always do good, it's inevitable that you'll end up doing something bad, that's how it works." She smiles.

"Thanks for telling me." Len laughs.

"So... I used my family's status to help out some bad people. Drug-smuggling, black market gambling... murder. I never really got involved in that side of things, though, that was my sister," Al explains reluctantly.

"What's your sister's name?" Len asks.

"Sonny." She smiles.

"Al and Sonny? You sound like a pair of badass gangsters." He laughs.

Al does, too and nods in agreement. "We *are* a pair of badass gangsters."

They smile at each other, feeling another, more passionate kiss coming on. Len decides it's enough for one night; he doesn't want to get too attached.

"We should get to bed. I've got a big day tomorrow." He slaps his hands onto his knees.

"You have! It's like Christmas came early." She smiles widely.

They embrace each other on the roof, the stars twinkling above them.

"I'm really going to miss you, Len," she says into his chest.

"I'm really going to miss you too, Al," he replies, stroking her hair gently.

CHAPTER FIFTEEN

The 6am alarm rings through the building and the bones of the patients, but today is different. Rather than having to drag themselves out of bed and stumble towards the shower rooms, everyone is in high spirits, jumping out of bed and springing down the corridor. Len says hello to everybody he passes on his way, including the nurses.

Everyone huddles around Len in the dayroom, wishing him well and asking him if he'll miss them all, to which he replies, "Of course I will!" to all of them.

Even DJ makes an appearance, his head wrapped in bandages. Len brings up what happened in the showers and DJ has no clue what he's talking about. "I only remember waking up in the morning," he explains.

Mehzah also comes down to see Len. Despite sharing a room with him, he still hasn't spoken to him in days.

"Lucky you, bru. I saw your plan in my comic. Good job you didn't go through with it, you'd be a dead man," he says to Len quietly.

Len blushes out of embarrassment. "I know. I wrote it out

of anger... There's no way I would have been able to defeat Atilla, anyway." He laughs. Mehzah does too, surprisingly.

The detectives turn up to oversee his release and finish up some business with the nurses about how they conduct their business in the hospital. Al spots them coming through the door, Detective Shelley's eyes lingering on her for long enough. She sneaks out of the group around Len and waltzes up the stairs to her room, where she passes Eucalyptus in the corridor,

"Oh hey, Al. Where are you going?" she asks.

"Just getting something from my room. Len's getting enough attention without needing me there." She laughs.

"I haven't seen him yet, so I'll head down now. I'll see you later." She squeezes Al's shoulder and dances down the stairwell.

Al sits down on her bed and awaits the arrival of her father patiently. It only takes him a couple of minutes to be directed to room 102 by Paul. He leaves the two of them alone immediately and returns to the staffroom.

"Oh, Alice." He breathes heavily and brings her in for a big hug. "I've missed you so much. I couldn't sleep at night from worrying so much," he tells her, as he grabs her soft hair in his hands and smells her head.

"I've missed you too, Dad," she reciprocates. "I'm coming home today, though. How's mum and Sonny?" She pushes away and smiles up at him.

"They're fine, hunny, they both miss you so much. Your sister can't wait for you to get home and back up to your old tricks again, she said, haha! We've got a party set up for you at home... God, I can't tell you how relieved I am to get you away from these crazy people."

"They're not crazy, Dad. And actually, there's something I need to ask of you. Things need to change in this hospital. The way they treat patients is disgusting."

"But what can I do?" he asks.

Whilst they have their heart-to-heart, Len can feel the absence of his dearest friend from the adoring circle.

"Where's Al gone?" he asks, looking around the huddle for her.

"Oh! I saw her going to her room!" Eucalyptus chirps, just happy to have helped.

"Do you mind if I go and have a minute alone with her?" he asks the group.

"Go for it, son!" Mr Lewis sings.

"Thanks, guys." He smiles, standing up.

The group disperses a little bit after he's left, but his favourites remain where they are for his return.

He slowly pops his head into the corridor, making sure there are no nurses or female patients that will catch him out being in a place he shouldn't be. The coast is clear. He tiptoes over to room 102. He can hear a pair of hushed voices so he peeks around the doorway and sees Al with Detective Shelley, standing close to each other, her arms grasped tightly in his hands.

"Please, Dad. It's an injustice not to act on this information!" she begs passionately.

Len's heart sinks to the floor and he freezes in fear. How did he not see this? Tears form in his wide, unblinking eyes. His breath becomes shallow and unhinged as he tries to process what he's just seen. Suddenly, his shock turns to anger. How could she? he thinks. His breathing becoming heavier and more agitated. His face contorts from desperation to pure contempt for everyone and everything in this shit hole.

"I promise, I'll see what I can do, darling," Shelley says.

"Thanks, Dad. I love you," Al replies.

Before he can get caught, Len picks himself up off the wall and stumbles angrily into the stairwell, hiding on the upper stairs. He hears a pair of loud, heavy footsteps and knows it's the detective. Once he's sure he's far enough out of the way, he storms back into the corridor and catches Al just about to leave her room.

"Len! Hi!" she stutters.

He doesn't reply, just looks at her angrily.

"What's up?" she asks, becoming more and more scared.

"You told him I killed Gaz, didn't you? Your *Dad*," He snaps.

"I didn't! I wouldn't do that to you, Len," she pleads. "I promise."

The words ring in his ears so familiarly. He slowly shuts the cell door, locking them both in the room.

Everybody groups together in the corridor, lining the path to the exit for Len. He walks through the middle, hugging his friends and shaking everyone's hand.

"It's been a pleasure, Len. Hopefully we'll see each other again, in another life. Hopefully at a party... full of drugs." Scott laughs, giving him a tight hug.

"Only if they're supplied by you." Len winks at him.

Len moves down one to meet eyes with Theo,

"It's been good," Len sighs.

"It has. We're gonna miss you," Theo says, going in for the hug.

"Keep practicing your poker face." Len smiles, patting him on the arm.

"My go next!" Eucalyptus grins.

"Of course, my favourite earth child," he says, as he plays with her hair a bit.

"Oh, Len. You're such a flirt!" She laughs as she pulls him in violently for a hug.

The wind is knocked out of him slightly but he laughs and moves on to Mr Lewis, still in his wheelchair.

"My dear boy. Don't forget what's happened here, what you've done for us all," Mr Lewis gushes, clasping Len's hands in his own.

"I won't, Mr Lewis."

"Give me a hand up, boy. I need to give you a proper farewell."

Len and Eucalyptus both help him up. At first he's a bit wobbly, but he soon regains his composure. A determined and respectful look flashes onto his face as his eyes narrow. He throws his hand up to his head in a big, grand salute and Len reciprocates with a smile on his face.

He's a few steps away from the door when he comes to Atilla and Adesso.

"I can't say we're going to miss you, Len," Atilla says.

"Good riddance, I say." Adesso rolls his eyes.

"I know we didn't get on. I just wanted to say thank you, for making me a man fit to be in the real world." He smiles, "I owe that to you and your beautiful facility here."

Atilla rolls her eyes but can't help smiling at his kind remarks.

"Good luck, Len." She shakes his hand.

"Thank you... Look after Al for me, will you?" He smiles.

He takes his first step onto the gravel path that leads to the road where his car waits for him. He breathes in the fresh morning air and the wet, earthly smell of the grass and smiles to himself. He turns around the face the hospital again and waves to his friends in the window – they're all still cheering for him. He blows a kiss to his fans one last time before he saunters up the path.

The nurses and the two detectives congregate back in the staffroom, telling each other how pleased they are that Len is gone.

"I think I'll quite miss him," Paul reminisces. "I liked his stories."

Atilla holds up a bottle of rum. "What do you say, some of this in your coffee?" She smirks. She pours an equal amount in everyone's mug and they add their cheers to Len's departure.

"And to Alice. We couldn't have done it without her!" The Dealer adds on.

"Where is Ace?" Adesso asks.

"She was in her room last time I spoke to her," Shelley mutters.

"Isn't it weird how he was always the one to kill the villain in his story, yet he never said that about the night of the murder," Paul wonders to himself out loud, ignoring the other conversation going on.

Shelley looks at Reinhold cautiously and, without having to say a word, they simultaneously rush to room 102, the nurses struggling to keep up behind them.

The door is closed when they get there. Shelley and Reinhold place a hand on their guns hidden under their blazers and slowly pry open the door. Inside, the crumpled body of a young woman sits in a pool of blood on the floor. Her blood is everywhere – on the beds, on the wall, even on the ceiling light. Shelley drops to his knees, tears already streaming out of his eyes. Reinhold, less emotionally attached, goes to check her pulse. Instead of feeling her soft, cold skin, his fingers land on a hard object, impaled in her neck. He slowly pulls it out, discovering it's a tortoiseshell, navy blue pen with the name *PAUL* written on it. His eyes snap to the young nurse who's standing open-mouthed in shock.

"Is this your pen?" he snaps angrily.

"Eh... Yeah, but I haven't seen it all week! The last time I had it was when Len arrived. I asked him to sign my book and... I never got it back," he suddenly realises.

Reinhold pushes past the ogling crowd and runs frantically to the main entrance. He makes it halfway down the stone pathway before the car speeds off, leaving nothing but a trail of dust in its wake.

Dear reader,

We hope you enjoyed reading *Len World*. Please take a moment to leave a review, even if it's a short one. Your opinion is important to us.

Discover more books by Isobel Wycherley at

https://www.nextchapter.pub/authors/isobel-wycherley

Want to know when one of our books is free or discounted? Join the newsletter at

http://eepurl.com/bqqB3H

Best regards,

Isobel Wycherley and the Next Chapter Team

You might also like:
Gone Too Far West by Isobel Wycherley
To read the first chapter for free, please head to:
https://www.nextchapter.pub/books/gone-too-far-west

ABOUT THE AUTHOR

I was born on the 13th of September, 1999 in Warrington, England.

I wrote my first book when I was eighteen, based around my experiences in the summer of 2018.

I study linguistics at Manchester Metropolitan University, I am interested in pursuing forensic linguistics and have an interest in acquisition.

I love music, it's always been a big part of my life, as well as helping me to establish a positive attitude towards anything. Films are another love of mine, which I try to reflect in my writing style, since I generally picture my stories as films playing out in my head, which helps me to imagine what I would want to see happen next, if it really were a film.

I'm very inquisitive and want to know everything about everything. I love learning and experiencing new things and I can't wait to see where that takes me, especially in my new writing career.

Len World
ISBN: 978-4-86747-065-7

Published by
Next Chapter
1-60-20 Minami-Otsuka
170-0005 Toshima-Ku, Tokyo
+818035793528

18th May 2021

Lightning Source UK Ltd.
Milton Keynes UK
UKHW040637271022
411161UK00001B/17